The W...

Charles Ki...
retold for the screen by
Michael Robson

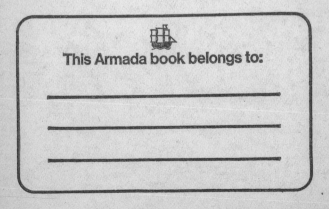

This Armada book belongs to:

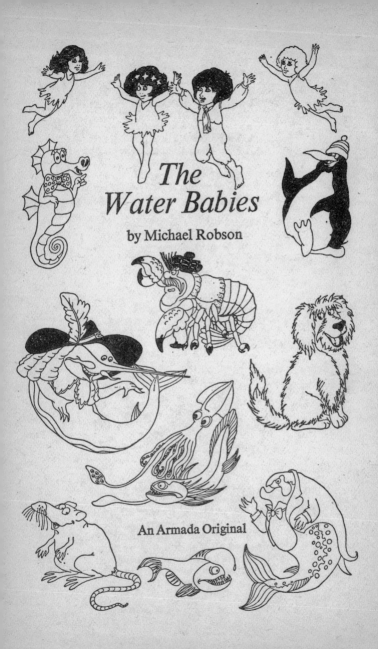

The Water Babies

by Michael Robson

An Armada Original

The Water Babies was first published in the U.K. in 1978
in Armada by Fontana Paperbacks, 14 St. James's Place,
London SW1A 1PS

© 1977 Ariadne Films Ltd. 1978
A Peter Shaw Production

Acknowledgement: The songs on pages 56, 58, 65–66, 81–82
and 117 are by Phil Coulter and Bill Martin. The lyrics on
pages 44, 50–51, 99–100 and 104 are by Michael Robson.

Printed in Great Britain by
Love & Malcomson Ltd., Brighton Road,
Redhill, Surrey

For Peter and Valerie Shaw

Contents

One
Tom and Friends

His name was Thomas Aquinas Something-or-Other, and he was in a terrible hurry. He had a little time off work, and he was anxious to fill it to his complete satisfaction. So there he was, bouncing and skipping and running through the crowded streets of one of the biggest, liveliest industrial towns that the noble county of Yorkshire could brag of in this year of grace 1850 – or something.

Tom was small for his age, which was about twelve, and extremely grubby. He was usually to be found dressed in a job lot of boots and tatters unwillingly given to him by his employer, Mr Saul Grimes. For Mr Grimes was a master chimney-sweep, and young Tom was his apprentice. It was Mr Grimes's aim to give Tom as little food and beer – for in those days small boys were allowed to drink beer since the water would have killed them – as would keep the lad alive. If he overdid the victuals, Tom would grow fat, and be quite unable to wriggle up those endless, narrow chimneys with his sticks and brushes. On the other hand, were Mr Grimes to supply Tom with no roof over his head and no food at all, the boy would die extremely quickly, and Mr Grimes would have no unpaid help to do the bulk of his work for him. So you can see that, for Mr Grimes, extremely careful judgment was needed in keeping his young apprentice fit for his job.

Having, as usual, an empty stomach, and no money, Tom stole what he fancied from the many stalls in the busy market town. He stole a piping hot mutton pie and half a pound of bananas, even though, had he been caught, he would have been flogged and transported to Botany Bay as quick as you like. Having eaten his breakfast and enjoyed it, Tom stopped briefly in the market-place to watch a prize-fight between two barefisted bruisers, to befriend a small, filthy dog called Toby, and to hear about the latest public hanging. In those days, life and death were close companions, and never less than interesting.

By and by, Tom and Toby were attracted by the sound of a small man thumping a very large drum. He stood in front of a large canvas booth, which bore on it the following interesting information: MADAME DOASYOU- WOULDBEDONEBY! THE HEAD WITHOUT A BODY! Since Tom was unable to read, he was obliged to make do with gazing in fascination at a lurid painting of an attractive golden-turbanned lady, without a body, and apparently enclosed within a glass dome! A head without a body! This was something Tom absolutely had to see! He left Toby in the cobbled street, and darted inside the great booth, easily avoiding the stern glare of the gentleman at the entrance, who was supposed to be taking pennies from those wishing to see this Oriental marvel.

Inside the booth, Tom joined the queue of marvelling, partly-drunk spectators. There was a strange, half-frightening, half-appealing smell all around. Had Tom but known it, the smell was an interesting compound of joss-sticks, sandal wood, faded jasmine, and two flickering oil-lamps, which gave off an odour more commonly associated with coaching-stations than an Eastern hideaway. But there was the beautiful lady's head, looking extremely healthy, and moving very slowly, now to the right, now to the left. By the time her eyes had chanced upon young Tom, he was the only spectator present. A yashmak – or gauzy veil – fell from the lady's face, and she favoured Tom with a slow wink. Tom, terrified, raced out of the booth, closely followed by Toby.

Had he but stayed on, encouraged rather than alarmed by the lady's friendliness, and had he edged around a little closer, he would have soon discovered that the attractive lady did in fact possess a perfectly normal body in an absolutely normal way. But by a clever use of matt black velvet and angled mirrors, the overall impression to anyone walking through the booth was that of a living, breathing face set inside a glass dome.

But Tom was racing off and away, heart pounding with fear and wonder. He bounded over the cobbles, head down, arms flailing and legs moving like urgent pistons – until he ran headlong into an obstacle. As Tom reeled, gasping, a dirty, calloused thumb and forefinger seized the boy's right ear and twisted hard, and a thick, deep Yorkshire voice enquired:

'Where was you off, then?'

No need for Tom to look up: his ear was fast in the grip of his master, Saul Grimes! The sweep lifted Tom up on high, until the apprentice's grubby face was less than two inches from Mr Grimes's own – and neither was a pretty sight.

Mr Grimes was a man of some sixty years; at least fifty-two of which had been spent drinking whatever form of alcoholic beverage he could lay his hands on. Although the day was bright, Mr Grimes wore an exceedingly long topcoat which just avoided brushing his bruised and reeking boots. Atop his dirty head he wore a tall and damaged stove-pipe hat, into the hatband of which some drinking crony had, many years previously, stuck a tall feather. The feather was bent and sad now, but Mr Grimes left it in his hat. He felt, obscurely, that it lent him a certain raffish distinction.

By his side was his inveterate companion, Mr Damiel Masterman. What Mr Masterman did for a living, no one was totally sure. Many suspected, and perhaps rightly, that he was a petty thief. Mr Masterman wore a threadbare military greatcoat from which depended a single medal. Some poor fellow had won it for valour in a terrible encounter with the French at Waterloo, but Mr Masterman had been no nearer Waterloo than the station which bore that name in the city of London. To add to the seedy military effect, Mr Masterman wore a grimy cap that had once belonged to a dashing young ensign in a crack cavalry regiment. Mr Masterman's face was pale; his eyes were pale; his hands were faintly purple. He was, all in all, not the kind of man you would wish to accompany your maiden aunt on a journey to Folkestone.

Grimes was addressing this insult to humanity even now, as the sweep studied Tom's far from bashful face.

'Did you ever see such *a* ungrateful wretch as this one, Mr Masterman?'

Mr Masterman glanced at the lad without pleasure.

'Can't say as I'd ever wish to, Mr Grimes,' he replied.

'What happens to 'prentices as dodge their masters, Damiel?' snarled Grimes.

'They're flogged and deported to Botany Bay, Saul,' Mr Masterman informed him dolefully.

Grimes shook Tom vigorously. 'You hear that, Thomas? Did you hear that, you whelp?'

He hurled Tom away from him. The boy bounced across the cobbles and almost immediately was on his feet again. He was neither hurt nor frightened; neither angry or amused. Such had been his treatment at the hands of the adult world all his short life. A boy either survived and thrived – or he died. Most died. A few, like Tom, managed to exist. He bent to pat the mongrel, who was busily examining him for broken bones, then looked up at his master.

'Work is it, Mister Grimes?'

Grimes nodded soberly (though he was far from sober).

'Aye – work. Very important work. An appointment at Harthover Hall!'

'High cockalorum, young Thomas!' said Mr Masterman.

'High cockalorum indeed, Mr Masterman,' chuckled the master-sweep; and all four made directly for the nearest public-house.

'High cockalorum' may be puzzling you. It was an expression indicative of pleasure or excitement. 'Fine and dandy,' you might have said had you been living in North America at this time. But in the great industrial cities of England, the noisier set were fond of employing the aforementioned expression. Tom knew it well, and it was 'high cockalorum' he was muttering to Toby as he saw Mr Grimes and Mr Masterman settle down at their customary table in the foul public bar of *The Hangman's Rest*. Because Tom knew from experience that once Mr Masterman had enjoyed five or six pints of beer, and once Mr Grimes had enjoyed a bottle or two of gin with hot water, both men would relax more than a little, and even condescend to offer Tom a swig of beer here, a sip of gin there, and sometimes a slice of tobacco.

Tom was despatched with fourpence to the counter, where he bought a can of gin for his master and a pint of ale for Mr Masterman. With the change that was left he bought some fresh bread, and the landlord, seeing the dog at his side, slipped the lad a bundle of bones. Soon Tom and Toby were squatting in the straw close to the men's table, sharing their bread and bones. Meantime, Mr Grimes and Mr Masterman were up to no good at all. Something was afoot, Tom could tell, even from the muttered scraps of conversation he was able to overhear.

'Aye, but it's dangerous, Damiel,' Mr Grimes was murmuring.

11

Mr Masterman took a deep draught of ale, then leaned over the table and spoke persuasively to his ally.

'Do you want to be a sweep all your life, Saul? Or a toff with a coach and four – and a pack of servants?'

'Or a snapped neck if they catch us!' said Mr Grimes, and casually snapped one of the burnt-out clay pipes that lay on the table beside him.

'You know what they say about Harthover Hall, don't you, Mr Grimes?' chirped Tom.

Alarmed, Grimes seized Tom by the throat

'WHAT do they say about Harthover? Speak, lad, afore I knock thy little eyes out!' he hissed.

Grinning, Tom surveyed the two anxious faces staring at him.

'Why, they say it's got more chimneys than you've given me hot meals, Mr Grimes!'

Relieved, Grimes flung Tom into a corner, and Mr Masterman chuckled at the boy's impudence. He poured some of his ale into a battered halfpint pewter pot, and, leaning over, handed it to Tom.

'Best get outside of that, lad – then go to sleep. It'll be a long day tomorrow!'

And a long day it certainly proved to be. Quite the longest in Tom's short life.

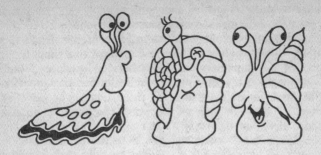

Two
Events at Harthover

Along the wet dark streets walked Mr Hickory, lamp-lighter and watchman.

'Four o'clock of a rainy morning!' he shouted. And four o'clock of a rainy morning it was; not the kind of morning any boy would rush out of bed to spring into. But since Tom had no bed and was no ordinary boy but a sweep's apprentice, he did not find it strange to be plodding along over the wet cobbles, carrying cleaning-rods and brushes over one shoulder. Behind him trotted Toby. Ahead of them ambled Wilfred, Mr Grimes's donkey. Wilfred was carrying an irritable but silent Mr Grimes, and a great many panniers and sootsacks also. Fortunately, Mr Masterman had remembered to feed and water Wilfred the night before, because without his daily rations, Wilfred was the most stubborn donkey ever to survive in a Northern industrial town. And even with his rations he was no angel.

In front of Wilfred walked Mr Masterman, sniffing miserably now and then, and occasionally, listlessly, rubbing at the ancient bugle which he was now carrying, slung over one shoulder.

They walked on and on, out of what seemed to be the township proper, and past slagheaps and collieries –

where women as well as men were working, and boys and girls of Tom's age also struggled for a livelihood. For this was what the sentimental might call 'Merrie England'; merry it may well have been for perhaps one thousandth part of the population at that time; for anyone, in fact, who possessed the means to live well and sleep comfortably. But for most of the people of those times, whether they lived in towns or villages, life was appalling and usually short. Freedom they may appear to have, by any number of ancient laws, but it was generally the freedom to die when they could work no longer or fight the countless diseases that poverty, filth and overcrowding bred amongst them.

Happily, Tom was unable to comprehend what an extraordinarily unfair world he lived in. What concerned him was only to exist from day's beginning to day's end with the minimum punishment from Mr Grimes, the minimum work he could manage to do, and the maximum food and drink he could beg or steal to keep his wiry little body together. From the age of perhaps six, Tom had learned the difficult art of walking in the right direction whilst still being nine-parts asleep. Consequently, when at last the miserable party left the ugly outskirts of the town behind them and headed into real countryside, Tom had not woken up.

The sun had appeared by now, and the morning mists were rising fast. Mr Masterman, unused to such exercise, was anxious to bathe his feet, and the sight of a clear and even sparkling stream was too much for him to resist. So he tore off his boots and, possessing no socks, plunged his legs and feet into the cold water.

Tom blinked as the sunlight dazzled him, then began to take in the unusual and beautiful scene about him.

'Hey, where's this then?' he piped.

Mr Grimes, who had slid off Wilfred and was sprawling on the wet grass, delved inside his stovepipe hat and came up with a small green bottle full of gin. To this he applied himself rigorously, then exhaled his breath and addressed Tom.

'Where's this, then? Where dost think it is – China? It's Yorkshire, tha great fool!'

'Aye, I know it's Yorkshire, Mr Grimes.'

'Well then!'

'But I never seen Yorkshire clean before.'

Mr Grimes sighed noisily at the ignorance of the boy.

'We're in the COUNTRY, lad, where there's nowt to make it dirty!'

'The country? Is that what they call it, Mr Grimes? Hey, it's lovely, isn't it!'

Mr Masterman was drawing on his boots. 'I shall retire here,' he said sonorously.

'Hold thy tongue!' Mr Grimes warned him. The master-sweep slumped on to Wilfred, and the procession was off on its way again, threading down a long goatpath towards the great estate of Harthover.

It was when they found themselves walking through mysterious belts of mist that Tom began to experience the same tingling sensation he had first felt when seeing Mrs Doasyouwouldbedoneby, the lady with only a head to boast of. The mist occurred in a steepish defile, through which the group of sweeps were making their way. Bracken overhung them, and all natural sounds were diminished.

And abruptly – so abruptly that Wilfred shied violently – an old hag appeared through the mist.

Tom shuddered convulsively.

She was quite the most repulsive old creature any of them had ever seen.

Blackened, stumpy teeth protruded from between thin and purple lips. Bleared eyes stared at them above wrinkled, hideously-scarred cheeks. Her hands, held out to Mr Grimes in apparent supplication, were like ancient tentacles.

With an oath, Grimes kicked out at her. The old hag, a great bundle of kindling slung over her humped back, fell heavily backwards into the sodden moss.

Mr Masterman scampered past her, sniggering nervously. Toby trotted forward to investigate her. Tom crept up and gingerly held out his grubby little hand to help her up. And the old hag smiled her gratitude.

The strange tingling thoroughly pervaded Tom's mind and body. Because, somehow, in those bleared and blood-shot eyes, he seemed to see the beautiful and limpid eyes of the strange Oriental lady in the booth – the lady without a natural body. Then she was again an old hag who mumbled something and shuffled off in the opposite direction to the track that led towards Harthover. And almost as soon as the hag reached the next strange belt of mist – she vanished. Utterly and completely! Tom stared and stared, then turned, and scampered off after his master.

It was eight o'clock by the time they reached the gates and lodge that proclaimed Harthover Hall.

Mr Sladd, a massive man who looked as if he could take on ten prize-fighters and eat them before breakfast, stumped out of the lodge and stared at Mr Grimes through the huge railings of the gate.

'What's your business!' he demanded.

'What's our . . . ? We've come to sweep the chimneys! What's it look like!'

Sladd's tiny eyes surveyed the cringing Mr Masterman. 'Thought you was the undertaker,' he said, addressing Mr Grimes once more. 'Going to bury him. He looks like the walking dead.'

Sladd was convulsed with the power of his own wit. Mr Masterman was seriously affronted. But Mr Grimes enjoyed the joke at his crony's expense, as did young Tom. Sladd pushed open one of the gates, and the sweeping party filed past him. They had gone perhaps ten yards when they heard him call: 'See you don't come out with more than you went in with!'

Mr Grimes and Mr Masterman froze in horror. What could Sladd possibly know of their plans? So sudden was the halt of the two men that Tom stumbled into the immobile Mr Masterman and backed off, coughing. That thin wretch turned round and smiled ingratiatingly at the keeper.

'What d'ye mean?' he asked, in uncertain tones. Sladd

strutted towards them, and stuck his thumbs inside his belt.

'We've got no time for poachers, lads. So think on!'

Mr Grimes and Mr Masterman exchanged glances of relief.

'Poaching? Perish the thought!' exclaimed Mr Grimes.

'Nasty suggestion!' cried Mr Masterman. 'Killing poor dumb beasts? Very nasty!'

'Just remember,' continued Sladd, unconvinced. 'Squire Harthover's a Justice of the Peace. And it's the gallows in these parts for fellows as takes what don't belong to 'em!' He nodded, then turned and trudged massively back to the lodge.

The broad path that led towards the Hall itself was well-weeded. Trees and bushes crowded over it, and the sun was hot where it pierced the green gloom. Birds darted and flashed through bars of sunlight. Tom was beginning to enjoy his outing. The three of them trudged on quietly until they had almost rounded a sweeping bend in the path. And once again Mr Grimes stopped – though this time in amazement rather than fear.

'By the Lord, Tom!' he croaked. 'There's a power of chimneys there!'

Tom, shuffling past Mr Grimes, saw that indeed there were a very large number of chimneys at Harthover Hall.

It was an intriguing rather than a beautiful building, and it appeared that every owner of the place had in turn added some folly of his own devising to the original house – which they tell me was quite a charming little place when it was first constructed not more than five hundred years ago. But now it was something of an architectural monstrosity, and above each and every successive addition, chimneys towered. Chimneys of fantastic shapes and sizes – so many that Tom realised he would not be able to count them all in a single day, let alone sweep them.

'I'll not be through with that lot before Christmas!' he gasped. And added, 'Next year!'

It was to the tradesmen's entrance that they made their

way now – no question of sweeps arriving at the main entrance, which was normally reserved for peers of the realm and occasional baronets. Mr Grimes rapped briskly on the door, then swayed. The gin he had drunk the previous night, coupled with what he had drunk en route to Harthover, had rendered him less than steady on his feet. Mr Grimes knocked again. The door was opened fast by a formidable lady known to the household as Mrs Tripp. She wore round, gold-framed spectacles, but when she looked at Tom her eyes were clear and dancing, and Tom felt, yet again, that odd tingling sensation. There was something about Mrs Tripp that instantly put him in mind of the strange and beautiful head in the glass dome, and the weird old hag whom Tom had helped to her feet not ninety minutes previously. But Mrs Tripp was now regarding Mr Grimes with an expression of grim intensity.

'What a disgusting, smelly disgrace to humanity you are,' she informed him.

'I'm Grimes, ma'am,' said Mr Grimes, lurching away from this formidable person a little.

'You're drunk, sir!'

'Nevertheless, I'm Grimes, ma'am,' he persisted. 'Now, do you want them chimneys swept or you do not want them chimneys swept?'

Mrs Tripp's severe glance embraced the three of them.

'Now listen to me – all of you! I've dust-sheeted all the rooms where the chimneys are to be swept. I see you've plenty of sootbags – so use them! Because I warn you; one speck of soot in any of the rooms, and not one penny piece shall you have from me!'

Awed, Mr Grimes raised his hat. Tom and Mr Masterman raised their caps.

'Yes, Ma'am,' all three quavered.

'Well – get on with it!'

Tom and Mr Grimes collected the sootbags from the paniers on Wilfred's back, Tom once again shouldered the cleaning-rods, and they were about to march off to begin work when Mr Masterman sidled up to Mr Grimes confidentially. The cadaverous gentleman laid his finger down the side of his nose and whispered to the master-sweep, 'I'll be outside, Saul – to collect the – ' Then he saw that Tom could hear him, ' – to collect the sootbags!' he corrected quickly. He vanished into the garden. Tom wished with all his heart that he, too, were going into that bright and beautiful place.

Mr Grimes led Tom into the vast dining-room, gripping him by the nape of the neck. This was always the most difficult part of it all, both for master and apprentice. Tom really hated scrambling up the insides of chimneys, and made a point of trying to bolt for it when the moment of ascent was near. Mr Grimes knew this – had he not himself clambered up chimneys for *his* master for eight years, until his shoulders grew too big to allow him entry? – and knew that Tom had to be dragged and kicked to his work. Once inside the terrible darkness, Tom worked very fast. All he ever wanted to do was to see the light of the sky again.

The great room was, as Mrs Tripp had promised, fully dust-sheeted; and all the carpets had been rolled into the centre of the room and covered with more sheets. Standing behind the door, the mysterious housekeeper watched Mr Grimes and Tom struggling by the chimney-breast. Neither knew she was watching them.

Mr Grimes thrust Tom's cleaning rod, with its big brush-head, into the boy's hand, and shoved him to the chimney.

'On yer way and earn yer keep,' he advised.

Tom, groaning, vanished into and up the chimney. Soot began to fall lightly.

'Hey, it's dark up here, Mr Grimes!'

'What didst expect, yer great ruffian?' Grimes bellowed, and to speed Tom on he jabbed at the boy's retreating bottom with a heavy poker. Tom bawled with pain and wriggled higher.

'Faster!' yelled Mr Grimes. 'Else I'll light a fire and roast thy backside for thee!'

'No fires, PLEASE, Mr Grimes!'

19

Mr Grimes laughed brutally and backed away from the fireplace. Distant thumpings indicated to his satisfaction that Tom was clambering up the chimney at some speed. Then the sweep became aware that Mrs Tripp was watching him icily. Mr Grimes's spirit quailed before that formidable person. He attempted to be chummy.

'Wonderful what a bit of kindness does for them young wretches, missus!'

Mrs Tripp sniffed pointedly, and swept out of the room.

Then Mr Grimes began to behave rather unusually. The moment he had satisfied himself that Mrs Tripp was well on her way to another part of the Hall, Mr Grimes closed the door, and walked very briskly across to where he judged the sheeted sideboard was. He drew away the dustsheet, and his hopeful eyes lit upon a fine selection of silver cutlery, ornaments and plate. With zest, speed and no little skill, Mr Grimes transferred the squire's silver into a sootbag, then re-covered the sideboard with the sheet. He paused once, and, for the benefit of anyone who might just have happened to be passing, called out in his silkiest and most charming voice:

'Faster, Tom, dear fellow! Mustn't spend all day on one chimney!'

Then he carefully searched the rest of the room for further silver or useful *objets d'art*, added all these to the growing pile in the sootbag, carefully placed filthy cloths to prevent the stolen property from rattling or being damaged, and strode to the window that overlooked the garden. He opened the window, peered around, and up. No one save an advancing Mr Masterman was about. Mr Grimes hurled the sack of booty into Mr Masterman's waiting arms, and closed the window quickly.

Mr Masterman rapidly vanished into shrubbery outside and hid the sack of stolen goods. Inside, Mr Grimes was once again at the chimney. He peered up, and a great ball of oily soot fell softly on to his face, utterly blackening it. Mr Grimes swore vigorously, sneezed, and retreated into the hearth.

Poor Tom, sneezing and whimpering, could by now see

a thin ray of light above him. He wriggled his sore elbows and toes hard, and continued climbing up. The last few yards, as he knew all too well, were the worst. If you lost your nerve and your grip, you could fall – and falling down a chimney in a house that size was no laughing matter. Sometimes young sweeps collapsed and suffocated within extensive chimneyworks, and Tom had no desire to end his days within the architecture of Harthover's walls. So he fought on and up, and eventually squeezed himself out of the chimney, and, blinking against the sudden glare of the sun, began to look about him.

Here was the whole irregular world of the rooftops – and a fascinating spectacle it presented. But for Tom, used hitherto only to city chimneys, it was the magnificent panorama beyond that delighted him. Lawns and kitchen-gardens and stables, little orchards and ornamental ponds, a great sweep of pasture, meadows where cows were grazing, and, far, far away, the glint and promise of a river. And trees! So many and such varied trees with all those subtleties of green that can perhaps only be found in an English landscape. Tom was enraptured.

Far below, in a long gallery, Mr Grimes strolled appreciatively and smiled to see the kind of beauty that *he* liked! More silver! Silver snuffboxes and silver cardcases. Silver framed miniatures and silver ornaments! How much would he and Mr Masterman be able to raise on this little lot? But Mr Grimes was quick to recall the apparent reason for their visit to Harthover – to clean the chimneys! Not far away, in a corridor beyond the gallery, was another chimney prepared and ready for the brushes. To this one Mr Grimes repaired. He knelt, and bellowed up into darkness:

'You should be done there by now!'

Up above, Tom was strutting about the hot roofs, thoroughly enjoying himself, and taking the sun like a grubby kitten. Up the chimney came his master's voice, weirdly distorted.

'Tom! Come on, lad! Down this way and sharp about it!'

Tom sighed, his brief freedom was over. He crossed to the closest chimney-stack and yelled down it:

'Righto, Mr Grimes! Coming down this one!'

With one last, longing look at the clean, green, beautiful parkland, Tom stepped into the chimney and began sliding down it. Unhappily, he had stepped into a more complex series of flues than he had ever encountered before, and soon his bottom came into contact with what, by experience, he judged to be a Y-junction, though in this case a Y upside down. Tom decided to move left and down. He fell and fell, choking and gasping.

All the time, Mr Grimes was transferring Squire Harthover's silver to yet another waiting sootbag with undeniable pace and *brio*.

Tom was falling, faster and faster, and below his naked feet he was pushing a ball of soot that grew ever larger, until at length the black ball emerged into a room in a part of the house that Mrs Tripp had clearly not dust-sheeted! The soot exploded gently in a white fireplace and floated outwards with a certain inky dignity. Tom followed fast behind it, and much less dignified was his descent. The boy was relieved and blind when he crawled out of the fireplace. Blind temporarily, to be sure, but blind nevertheless with soot. He wiped away as much as he could, blinked, and sneezed loudly. His eyes watered, and this washed the remainder of the soot away.

What he saw before him filled him with awe and anxiety.

For he was in the whitest bedroom – not that he had ever *seen*, since he had never seen anything remotely resembling a white bedroom – but that he could ever possibly have even *imagined*. The wallpaper was white. The carpet was white. The rugs were white. The curtains were white. The coverlet of the bed was white. The pillows were white – and the face of the little girl now looking at him in utter bewilderment from the bed was also white – but white with shock and fear. Her hair, which was very long, was so fair as to be almost white. Only her great big eyes were china-blue, and they were very wide now.

Tom was as surprised as the little girl for a moment, then his wits returned.

'Don't shout,' he pleaded. 'Please! I'm only the chimney-sweep . . . I come down the wrong chimney, see.'

The girl frowned. Then she saw the sooty footsteps that led from the chimney and fireplace to the centre of the formerly spotless carpet. She simply could not comprehend that anyone . . .

'You've come down the chimney, boy?'

Tom nodded.

'But how terrible for you! Aren't you frightened, being up there in the dark?'

Tom tried a bit of a swagger, but somehow he realised that this extraordinarily beautiful little girl deserved the truth.

'Well, sometimes I'm frightened up there – but I'm more scared of Mr Grimes. He's my master.'

'Mr Grimes?'

'Yes. He's my master – and he clouts me.'

'Clouts you?'

'Hits me,' Tom explained. 'Hits me regular – across the ear.'

'But what for?'

'What for?' Tom tried a joke. 'For nothing. I don't pay him to hit me!'

This sally was entirely lost on the girl. 'But if he keeps on hitting you, why don't you tell your parents?' she asked. 'They'd soon stop him.'

'Parents?' asked Tom.

'Your mother and father,' the girl explained patiently. 'Why don't you tell them he hits you, this Mr Grimes?'

'Aint got no Mum and Dad,' Tom replied. 'Never did have. Mr Grimes says I was hatched out in a London gutter by the sun.'

The girl thought about this for a time. It was almost beyond her comprehension.

'You got a Mum and Dad?' said Tom.

'No.'

'Ah.' And Tom nodded sagely, assuming that, after

all, perhaps most small boys and girls were like him in having no parents.

The girl, sensing something of what was passing through his mind, said, 'My mother and father died in Vienna last year, whilst they were on holiday.'

'Rum sort of holiday – to die on it. Anyway, where's Vienna?'

'It's in Austria.'

'Austria? Isn't that where they send the convicts?'

'I don't know what you're talking about.'

Tom realised he was getting into deep waters. 'Well,' he said, 'if you aint got no Mum or Dad, who looks after you, then?'

The girl brightened. 'My uncle and aunt – Sir John, and Lady Harriet.'

Tom was deeply impressed.

'Blimey! Royalty!'

'This is their house,' the girl explained.

Tom looked once again round the exquisite room, recognising the luxury explicit in it. 'Then they must be worth a few bob, your uncle and aunt,' he allowed. 'Paradise, this place is. My idea of Paradise.'

His attention was taken by a small wooden crucifix which was fixed to the wall nearest the window. Tom was intrigued and baffled, and walked across to it.

'Here,' he said, 'what they do that to him for? Who is he?'

'Jesus,' said the girl, astonished at Tom's ignorance.

'Who?'

'God.'

Tom nodded thoughtfully. 'Oh. Then he's got the right room, ain't he? Paradise, I mean.'

The girl smiled. There was something so refreshingly direct about this quaint boy, and something quite confident, too.

'What's your name?' she asked.

'I'm Tom, Miss. Er, Thomas Aquinas Something-or-Other.'

'Something-or-Other?'

'Well, you see,' Tom explained, 'you don't get a last name if you aint ever had no Mum or Dad – it's the rules. So really I'm just Tom. Never could get on with that Aquinas.'

'It's a very strange name, certainly,' the girl agreed.

'But what're you called?' Tom asked her.

'I'm Ellie.'

'Ellie! Well, that's a pretty name, that is, Miss – highly classy. But then it would be, you living here and all. I mean, you'd never be a Gert or a Ruby, living here.'

From somewhere beyond Ellie's bedroom there came a sudden crash. Ellie looked anxiously at Tom.

'What was that?'

'Dunno.'

'Please find out,' Ellie begged him. 'Noises aren't allowed in this house.'

Proud to be of service to the wholly delightful Ellie, Tom made straight for the door.

'Tom!'

The boy turned inquiringly, pleased she had remembered his name.

'Be careful,' she cautioned him.

With a manly swagger, Tom opened the door and entered the landing. What he saw puzzled him not a little. Mr Grimes, on his hands and knees, was hastily replacing certain silver articles in the sootbag, which had very clearly just dropped off the great mantelpiece. Mr Grimes started guiltily as Tom approached:

'Mr Grimes – what are you doing? Thieving?'

And hard on this question came the voice of Mrs Tripp.

'Ellie? Are you all right?'

Mr Grimes thought very fast indeed. (I promised you he was an interesting gentleman.) The swag was now bundled up inside the sootbag, and, as Mrs Tripp entered the gallery, Mr Grimes was already hurling the sack at Tom. The boy caught it unwittingly as Mrs Tripp was just about able to see what was going on. In horror, Tom dropped the bag to the floor. It fell open, disgorging soot and stolen articles of silver.

'What's going on here?' cried Mrs Tripp, advancing rapidly.

Mr Grimes recovered his wits very smartly, and stabbed an accusing finger at Tom.

'Why, you young thief!'

Tom was understandably staggered.

'What d'you mean, Mr Grimes?'

Mrs Tripp was very close now, and shouted, 'Grab him! Seize the young monster!'

Grimes started for Tom. Then Ellie appeared.

'No,' she called.

Mr Grimes was very close to Tom at this moment, but somehow Mrs Tripp appeared to interpose herself between master and apprentice. Grimes stumbled, in an attempt to avoid the angry housekeeper, and as Mrs Tripp swept the bewildered Ellie into her arms, Tom darted away from his master, and leaped to the nearest open window.

'Stop thief!' bellowed Mr Grimes.

'Stop thief!' commanded Mrs Tripp.

Ellie struggled to free herself from the tight embrace of the housekeeper. Tom took one last look round, then glanced below him.

Outside there was a great wisteria bush, whose gnarled old branches stretched far up beyond the window in which Tom crouched. As Mr Grimes clattered towards him, Tom leaped cleanly out of the window, and it seemed to those watching that here was a boy intent on breaking his neck, for the drop below was some forty feet.

Ellie screamed.

Tom fell

Three
The Moorland Chase

Mr Grimes, Mrs Tripp and Ellie are at the window, looking down. Two of them have very real fears that the lad will break his neck.

Tom is in a state of fall, turning over and over with delightful grace, but always aware, if only intuitively, that a falling object accelerates at a rate of thirty-two feet per second per second for quite a long time, provided that nothing intervenes en route. Tom is rather hoping that a branch of the wisteria will intervene, and fast!

Meantime, a word or two about Sir John and his wife, the Lady Harriet, because these important and basically charming people are going to have a direct bearing upon Tom's subsequent adventures.

Sir John Harthover was born John Harthover in the County of Yorkshire in the Year of Our Lord 1790. After undergoing an excellent classical education at Eton, John proceeded to the University of Oxford, where he did very little work, consumed a great deal of quite good wine, and came away with a degree without having taken a Final Examination to prove his worth. In those days, gentlemen did not take final Public Examinations – only Commoners were obliged to undergo that boring ritual. Young John, being the oldest son of his father the Baronet Sir Nigel, had only two occupations open to him: the Church, and the Army. And since young John always lost his place in the prayer book during Matins, he thought he would do a deal less damage in the Army than the Church. So John's father bought him a commission in a crack cavalry regiment. John saw action against Napoleon Bonaparte's armies in Spain and Belgium, and was present at the Battle of Waterloo, where it is reported he fought with vigour and ignorance.

When old Sir Nigel died, the title and the lands at Harthover passed to John, who became Sir John immediately, in accordance with British custom. Now the new Sir John did not wish to be an absentee landlord, so he resigned his commission most honourably, and hurried back to Yorkshire. Here he became a diligent landlord and squire. He knew the names and family situations of every tenant and employee at Harthover, and he was widely regarded as a charming, kindly and hardworking baronet.

By 1842, Sir John was in full control of his estates, and was feeling rather lonely in the great Hall at Harthover. At a ball one evening he made the acquaintance of the delightful Lady Harriet, only daughter of the Earl of Trincomalee. The acquaintance blossomed into friendship, and the friendship into love. In February, 1843, they were married. To their regret, they had no children, but they made much of little Ellie, who was the only daughter of Sir John's youngest brother, Harry. It came to pass, several years later, that whilst Ellie was staying with Sir John and Lady Harriet at Harthover, her mother and father travelled to Austria for a holiday. Tragically, they took certain waters, believing them to be good for their health. In the event, both Harry and his wife contracted cholera, and died in Vienna. So Ellie became Sir John's ward, and no child could have had more loving, helpful or eccentric guardians than Sir John and Lady Harriet.

Lady Harriet had the sweetest of natures, but she had never received much in the way of education, formal or informal, and she was inclined to be vague. She was sometimes known to attend masked balls without a mask, or to go riding without changing into her riding habit. Yet all who knew her loved her, including her little niece Ellie.

On that fine bright morning then, whilst Tom was dropping fast towards a branch of the wisteria, and Mr Grimes and Mrs Tripp were bellowing 'Stop thief!' out of an upper window, Sir John was in his study and Lady Harriet was in her bedroom. The study was below the window from which the cries were emanating, and the bedroom was directly above. Almost immediately, Sir John and Lady Harriet appeared at their respective windows – Sir John looking up, and Lady Harriet looking down.

'What is it, Mrs Tripp?' Sir John asked.

'What is it, Mrs Tripp?' Lady Harriet enquired.

'I have just said that, dear heart,' Sir John called up to his wife.

'So have I, dear,' Lady Harriet called down. 'What is it, Mrs Tripp?'

'A thief, milady,' said Mrs Tripp. 'Pinched the silver, milady!'

Lady Harriet was bamboozled. '*Pinched* the silver? Really?' She stared down past Mrs Tripp's head, to the upturned face of her anxious husband.

'What's *pinched*, dear?'

'Purloined, my love,' Sir John called. (He was not a JP for nothing). 'Someone has purloined the silver!'

'God save the mark!' cried Lady Harriet. 'This is perfectly frightful! Call the Justice of the Peace, John. Stop thief! Call the Justice!'

'I *am* the Justice, sweeting!' Sir John assured her. And he clambered out of his study window, crying loudly, 'Stop thief!'

In the gallery above, Ellie was breaking away from the tight hold of Mrs Tripp.

'It wasn't the boy, Mrs Tripp!' she cried. 'It wasn't Tom. It really wasn't! He isn't a thief! It was that wicked old man, Mr Grimes!'

'Nonsense, Ellie,' said Mrs Tripp, 'I saw him with my own eyes!'

Mr Grimes himself, that artful felon, had by now burst out of the main doors and was hurrying up the drive.

'Masterman!' he called.

Mr Masterman, who had just concealed the most recent bag of valuables and was remembering urgent appointments in Budleigh Salterton in view of the terrible excitement raging around the Hall, reluctantly showed his head above some laurels.

'You called, Mr Grimes?' he piped.

'Find that boy, Mr Masterman!' his accomplice instructed him. 'He's been a-stealing of the Squire's property!'

It did not take the deep-dyed villain Masterman long to realise the implications of his crony's advice.

'Quick as you like, Mr Grimes!' he called, and began to spring in the direction taken by Tom.

At this stage of the game, it's only fair to tell you that Tom, whilst falling, managed to grab hold of a friendly branch of the wisteria. Down this he wriggled, then dropped some six feet to soft soil in the flowerbed immediately below him. Hearing the hullabaloo all round, Tom decided to make a break for it away from the Hall. He ran with enormous zest for where he judged the wall to be. Attempting to intercept him were the gardener and the butler. But Tom was faster and neater than they. The gardener was approaching from Tom's right, and the butler from Tom's left. Tom feinted a retreat, then accelerated hard. Gardener and butler collided heavily and fell backwards, bellowing with rage and pain – their heads sagging in a bed of nasturtiums. But Sir John was not far behind, and although he was no longer in the first flush of youth, his great height and long legs enabled him to cover the ground – if only

30

for a short time – much faster than could Tom. The boy, seeing this, veered sharply towards the wall that marked the immediate perimeter of the Hall. Bushes and branches lashed at his face and naked legs and feet, but he sprinted on. Then Toby appeared, and shot across Sir John's path in his excited attempt to catch up with Tom. Sir John stumbled over the dog. Toby yelped. Sir John fell headlong and very heavily. This respite enabled Tom to shin up a friendly tree and gain the wall's top. He looked about him, then rapidly dropped over the outer side of the wall, and his feet touched the rough bracken of the great moor.

Sir John struggled, panting and grubby, to his feet. 'He shan't escape!' he shouted. 'I shall find him and make an example of him! We'll hunt the young scoundrel across Yorkshire if necessary!' He began to stride back towards the Hall, crying, 'To horse! To horse!'

Inside Harthover Hall, events were also moving rapidly. Ellie was by now fully dressed in her riding habit – without the apparent knowledge of Mrs Tripp. Ellie raced down the large circular staircase and, as she reached the foot, Mrs Tripp emerged from one of the upper rooms.

'Come back, Miss Ellie! Come back at once!'

But Ellie, headstrong, and sure of her intentions, reached the front door and ran outside. Had she remained within doors, she might have been very surprised indeed. For the formidable face of Mrs Tripp was now relaxing into an expression of mystical serenity. She crossed to the nearest window and looked out. From this angle she could just see a small section of moor, and no more. But she seemed to know that Tom was out there, running like a boy determined to *sprint* a Marathon.

'Run boy, run,' whispered Mrs Tripp.

And Tom, stumbling then straightening, and racing on, thought he could hear, somewhere deep down in his innermost soul, a strange, encouraging voice urging him:

'Run boy, run!'

All Harthover had been alerted. When a posse came thundering up the side drive, the heavy iron gates were opened, not without difficulty, by Mr Wadger, the East Lodge-keeper. Mr Wadger was old and rather deaf, but his wife had persuaded him that, since the Squire and all able-bodied riders were turning out in pursuit of the criminal, it behoved Mr Wadger to let the pursuers out. When Sir John, on a fine and mettlesome grey, reached the end of the drive, the gates were open. He nodded his thanks to Mr Wadger and urged his horse on. Mr Sladd followed on an extremely strong chestnut – the only horse in the stables sturdy enough to bear his weight – and a rag, tag and bob-tail of mounted retainers galloped after them.

Some way behind the rest of the pursuers came Mr Grimes and Mr Masterman. The master-sweep, never a man to indulge in energetic activity if there might be a way round it, had taken his cue from Sir John. Not possess-ing a horse of his own, Grimes had the next best thing – a sturdy donkey. So Mr Grimes urged Wilfred on after the horsemen. Mr Masterman trotted behind, from time to time blowing his ancient bugle, much to the irritation of Mr Grimes.

Mr Wadger watched them go with evident relief, then he slowly began to close the two iron gates. To his surprise, however, he heard a sound of further hooves pounding along the drive, and, looking up, he saw that Ellie, riding a fleet bay, was almost on top of him!

'God bless my soul!' he exclaimed, and darted to one side as Ellie and her bay raced past him. 'Miss Ellie on a pony? Dang me if I didn't think she were still a babby in swaddling clothes!'

Tom had not made directly across the moor from the place where he had landed over the wall. With all the in-stincts of a fox, and some of its hunted appearance, he had thought quickly, then decided to run *alongside* the wall for fully a quarter of a mile, until it curved back and made at a rather alarming angle for the Hall. Then Tom, seeing good running ahead, and a stand of timber not a furlong away, took to his heels. Toby, of course, picked up his trail almost immediately, so that by the time Tom entered the wood, the dog was lolloping by his side, greatly enjoying this wholly unexpected exercise. But it was Toby's appearance that dictated Tom's next course of action. Had the dog not picked up his scent and followed him, Tom would have been inclined to penetrate deep into the wood, then shin up a tree until he could find a suitable fork to relax in, and let the brouhaha pass by. But once Toby had reminded him how easily he could be followed, poor Tom dared not remain long in the deep shadows of the wood. He had visions of bloodhounds belling and howling after him, so he achieved the far side of the wood and raced on, hoping to find running water in which he might baffle any canine pursuers.

Ellie was riding very well indeed. She took hedges and walls like a champion, although her regular riding did not include such possible hazards. But her pony was young, and his stride was much shorter than those of the larger horses well ahead – he could never hope to catch them up. Nonetheless, Ellie kept him at it; somehow or other she *had* to speak to her uncle and Mr Sladd and the others before Tom was forced into something desperate. It was not very long before she reached those two perfidious wretches Mr Grimes and Mr Masterman. So astonished was Wilfred at her swift passage that he bucked hard, and Mr Grimes was unseated. He fell heavily, but the drop was short. Lying in the grass, Mr Grimes adjusted his stovepipe hat and felt for his secreted bottle of gin. He gazed after Ellie malevolently.

'I hope that nag throws her and breaks her neck!' he growled.

Mr Masterman, who was gasping for breath and looking thoroughly out of sorts, was surprised by the venom in his friend's voice.

'How's she crossed you, Saul?'

Mr Grimes took a revivifying drink of gin, gasped, and said, 'She saw me toss the swag at Tom. If she can convince the Squire, then it's . . .' And here the master-sweep did a fair imitation of a neck snapped by the hangman's rope.

Mr Masterman shuddered. 'If that's the case,' he stammered, 'we'd best clear off! I might look like a fox, but by cracky I don't want to die like one!'

Mr Grimes nodded, replaced the gin inside his hat, and hauled himself to his feet. His soot-rimmed eyes searched the horizon. 'Best get back to town as soon as we can,' he decided. 'They'll not find it so easy to track us down there, supposing the young wench *does* tell on me to Squire.'

Tom had been running for a very long time now, and he was exhausted. His mouth and throat felt as though warm charcoal was glowing there, and his legs were beginning to buckle. He was simply unused to this kind of cross-country dash, and his lungs, half-full of soot, could not make use of the air he was gulping down into them. All in all, he was in a very bad way, and felt extremely light-headed. In fact, aside of the stitch, and the ache in his lungs and legs, he felt very much as he often did when he had stolen just one gulp of gin too many from Mr Grimes's can – giddy and sick.

But ahead of him he thought he could hear the sound of rapidly-flowing water. Water! Water to drink and plunge his hot and dirty little body into! Water to shake off his pursuers! Tom staggered on another twenty yards, and found himself atop a bluff.

Trees and bushes led the way to a great racing river, and some two hundred feet below and to his left was a water-fall, overhung by a vast, flat rock. The water in the pool below it was so deep that it seemed black. Away beyond all this, Tom could see farmsteads dotted about, hazy in the shimmering, dancing air of noon. He could even discern that the river below him seemed to join a much larger river some miles away – a river that was lost in shining distances.

But it was the gurgle and plunge of water that was fascinating Tom. He needed that water, but he felt he had not the strength to take another step, let alone negotiate the tricky and dangerous descent to the great pool. The boy sank to his knees and groaned. Toby whined, and nuzzled into him to try and lick his fifthy, sweat-stained face.

Then both of them heard the sounds of pursuit!

Tom turned and saw, not two hundred yards away, Sir John and Sladd riding fast towards him. Scattered beyond them, and coming up rapidly, were perhaps eight or ten other riders. Tom rose to his feet, quivering with tension and fatigue. It was Toby who gave him the courage to act. He realised that the noisy objects coming at them very fast meant no good at all, and without hesitation the mongrel leaped over the edge of the bluff. Tom gave a shout and peered down. Toby had already landed, and was looking up at the boy and wagging his tail briskly. Tom eased himself over the edge, then his chimney-climbing proved its use. He was able to find toe- and hand-holds that no normal person could ever hope to use, but Tom's tough small hands and toes were used to this kind of effort. Soon the boy had reached the track below, and Toby was jumping up and down at him, barking excitedly.

By the time Sir John and Sladd had dismounted and looked down, Tom and Toby were making for light undergrowth that would hide them from view. Sir John and Sladd, knowing the area very well, went on foot to an easier path that would bring them close to where Tom appeared to be heading. But both men were panting as they slipped and slithered down the uneven path that must surely lead them to their prey.

Within five minutes Tom had reached the long flat stone and was standing on it. Below him, the river plunged and foamed in the great pool, then flowed on, broadening out under huge skies with only dim white puffballs of clouds to break the endless blue.

Sladd and Sir John had crossed the river by stepping-stones, and now, as they broke through undergrowth, they saw to their dismay that Tom had taken Toby into his arms, and was on the very edge of the slab of rock, and poised to leap down into the dark and sinister pool.

'Come back! Get back, lad!' Sladd shouted. 'You'll fall in!'

Sir John gasped in astonishment, and murmured, 'Good Heavens! He may be a thief, but he's a plucky little fellow! GET AWAY FROM THERE, BOY!'

Tom looked across, and saw that Sladd was stripping off his jacket, presumably preparatory to swimming across the narrower part of the river upstream of the great pool.

'What shall we do, Toby?' the boy whispered.

'Uncle John!'

Sladd and Sir John looked up in horror. Far above them, on the edge of the bluff, was Ellie, still in the saddle. If the pony were to lose its footing . . . !

'Get away!' yelled Sir John. 'Get away from the edge!'

'You must bring him back!' called Ellie, not moving. 'It wasn't Tom who stole the silver – it was his master!'

Tom's heart raced with pleasure that Ellie should have gone to such extremes to bear out his innocence. But then his attention was diverted to something else. Silently, Sladd had crossed the river, and was now moving, or rather, squelching, towards Tom. The boy moved to the very edge of the rock, and began to sway.

'Don't jump, lad! It ain't called Dead Man's Pool for nothing!' Slowly, the dripping Sladd advanced towards the nervous boy.

Then Tom felt again that extraordinary tingling sensation. He looked across the river and into the greenery beyond. There, dressed entirely in black and with a black hat and veil on, was the lady from the booth, the old hag, Mrs Tripp – all somehow merged into a pale but serenely beautiful face. The mysterious lady nodded pleasantly, and Tom knew what he must do. As Sladd reached the great slab of rock, Tom tucked Toby even more securely under his arm – and jumped out and down . . .

'Tom! Tom!' screamed Ellie.

Sladd gained the edge of the rock and looked down. Tom hit the dark surface of the water with a deep splash. Great gouts of water went everywhere. And boy and dog were sinking, sinking, sinking rapidly into that sinister pool from which no one had ever emerged alive.

Four
Underwater!

As he plummeted down and down, with bubbles streaming from his mouth, Tom felt certain he could hear, very clearly, the agonised voice of Ellie crying after him, 'Tom! Tom! Come back! Come back!' But he was so absorbed in what was happening to him and around him, that he forgot about the events that had led to his apparently fatal leap into the pool. Because first of all, *he was having absolutely no difficulty in breathing, even though he was by now thirty feet under water!* And secondly, though he seemed to be buoyant, he was not bouncing up to the surface like a cork, which the worried but hopeful Sladd was expecting him to do.

No. This small wiry boy was doing nothing that small wiry boys could in general be expected to do, and there seems to be only one explanation for this. The mysterious lady whom Tom had briefly seen in the undergrowth must have had certain special powers which enabled young Tom to undergo what we might call a 'sea change' – a change so radical and so unexpected that it was without precedent in the recorded history of the human race. For, as well as being able to breathe underwater without any artificial aids whatsoever, *Tom was beginning to shrink!* And by the time he actually touched bottom, some sixty feet below the surface of the pool, Tom was slightly less than half his earthly size. In fact, he was now a mere one foot ten inches high – though at first he had no knowledge of this, especially as Toby had shrunk in proportion, and was also well able to breathe underwater.

But the fact sadly remains that, since that time, only Tom and Toby have ever undergone this experience and survived to tell the tale, so that on no account should any enterprising young boy or girl or puppy EVER TRY THIS EXPERIENCE. Because they will surely end up stone dead very quickly indeed.

The bottom of the pool was agreeably firm, and Tom was in no discomfort whatsoever as he gazed about him in wonder. Fortunately, his shirt and breeches had accommodatingly shrunk to fit him exactly, and it was while looking at these articles of clothing that Tom caught sight of his hands and arms. And he was absolutely flabbergasted, because they were utterly –

'CLEAN! I'm CLEAN!' he shouted excitedly. And his voice rang out very healthily indeed. No problems here about speaking underwater.

Then Toby came paddling towards him, wagging his tail, and Tom realised that the dog was also utterly clean as well. This was astonishing! He and Toby had a bit of a cuddle, congratulating one another on their pluck and skill, then Tom tried to get up and move about. He found himself upside down and floating lazily into the side of the river. Toby, who was managing to move in this new element very well indeed, looked at the boy enquiringly.

For ten minutes Tom tried to swim, but failed miserably. Toby found his antics very entertaining, but Tom was less than amused. Then a shoal of minnows flashed past his face, tittering. They abruptly turned and moved down towards him with great curiosity.

'What's the matter with you?' they asked, in clear high voices.

'I can't swim!' said Tom, floundering badly. The minnows flickered round, examining this strange new creature inquisitively.

'Can't swim? But you're underwater, aren't you?'

By now Tom was standing upright, but feeling uncertain of his balance. Three toads, attracted by the commotion, flopped across and peered closely at Tom from their bulging eyes.

'He's underwater, yes. But what *is* he?'

'Yes, what *are* you?' squeaked all the minnows.

'I'm Tom!' And once more, Tom lunged forward in an attempt to move gracefully.

The minnows darted away, but at that moment two eels poured down to investigate, and spoke in deep and booming voices.

'A Tom? What's a Tom?'

The eels slithered round and round Tom until he became quite dizzy with trying to speak to them both at once.

'I'm a Tom!'

The first eel looked at him. 'Don't think much of that, for a start.'

A couple of watersnails glided up, and spoke to the

irritated eels in clear, bleeping voices. 'The trouble is that he can't swim,' they announced.

'He can't swim?' cried the eels incredulously.

'I can't swim!' shouted Tom, who was by now upside down and flailing amongst weeds.

Two rats swam fast across the area, disturbed by these statements.

'Queerest thing I ever heard – '

'If you can't swim good, you shouldn't be here!'

The minnows flicked round Tom's head, shrilling:

'Birds of the air can fly, fly, fly!'

'Four-legged friends can run, run run!' boomed the eels.

'And everything that lives in the water *has* to be able to swim!' declared all the creatures near Tom.

'Well I can't! SO!' yelled Tom, who was now very upset and angry, and also, if the truth be told, a little tearful. There was no way in which he could co-ordinate himself into making any sort of a show at swimming.

The water-creatures sensed his inner unhappiness; they were not, after all, naturally vindictive. So they all tried to explain to Tom how it was done. The toads, the minnows, the rats, the eels and the snails all tried – but without success. In fact, Tom became even more baffled than ever, since all the creatures just mentioned, being fashioned entirely differently, had quite different methods of propelling themselves through the water. So Tom eventually collapsed in a heap on the river bed, and looked wretched. Toby paddled across to comfort him.

Then a deep, quivering angry voice thundered across the scene, and every creature except Tom and Toby sprang to attention.

'Never been able to swim? Absolute nonsense!'

And there, advancing at great speed, were two great salmon – Ralph and Wilhelmina. Ralph wore an interesting cutaway coat, white shirt, white bow tie, and a monocle in his right eye. His lady wife Wilhelmina wore a salmon-pink evening dress and a nice line in earrings. Both were in their middle age, powerfully built, autocratic and really rather noble.

'Well, little newt,' Ralph began.

'I'm not a newt!' hissed Tom.

'Speak when you're spoken to!' said Wilhelmina grandly.

Humbled, Tom stood straight, and held his thumbs in line with the seams of his trousers.

'Without standards, we are lost!' said Ralph emphatically. 'Absolutely lost. And to keep up the standards here, my lady wife and I shall have to undertake to teach you to swim.'

Tom became so excited that he forgot his military stance and began hopping up and down with anticipation. Because he felt that if anything in the world could help him, it would be these two magnificent creatures. Indeed, Tom thought there was a certain fleeting resemblance between Ralph and Sir John Harthover.

'Will you really?' he squeaked.

'A salmon's as good as his word,' Ralph told him nobly.

'And you'd better believe it,' Wilhelmina added.

Ralph adjusted his white tie, and proceeded to the

centre of the pool bottom. A muted fanfare sounded.

'Clear the floor!' commanded the great salmon. And at once there was a flurry of activity and excitement such as Tom had rarely seen before. The water creatures moved so fast and efficiently that they blurred before his eyes. The whole effect, though Tom could not have known this, was like that of being in a theatre with a revolving stage. Lights are changing, the scenery is turning, some sets are being flown and others are being neatly lowered – all is purposeful and exciting activity.

Music began. It came from a group of Water Rats who were now sitting on a small daïs, with music-stands in front of them. Two of them had unusual violins, and a third was seating himself in front of a large piano of the kind more often found in the ballrooms of great liners than on the bottom of a very deep Yorkshire pool. Pale pillars gave a brilliant suggestion of a ballroom also, and above them all, very high indeed, was a vast and elaborate candelabra. The sun, refracted down through the deep waters, managed to hit the crystals, and light bounced and rained everywhere – gleaming, verdant, sensational!

Several coypu (who had no business being there at all since no one intended to bring them to England for almost a century yet) were acting as waiters. They wore charmingly-striped aprons, and each carried a snowy napkin with which he flicked imaginary dust from imaginary tables. The water-snails now looked like liveried flunkeys, and those two boomers, the eels, were dressed to the nines with black evening clothes and bright sashes. The toads wore rather garish hound's-tooth checks and smart brown boots with spatterdashes. A sly, raffish-looking water rat abruptly appeared between the centre rear arches, and placed a bugle, not unlike the one favoured by Mr Masterman, to his lips. From the bugle there came clear and gladsome notes. The fanfare was filched from an obscure work by Mr Offenbach: how the bugler had obtained a copy of the music, no one cared to ask.

Then the bugler stood to one side and stiffly to attention. Ralph and Wilhelmina, fin in fin, strode majestically to

42

the centre of the ballroom. Ralph bowed, and Wilhelmina curtsied. The music moved into a waltz tempo, and the two noble salmon began to move with dexterity and grace round the ballroom. Tom was delighted, and could have watched for hours. The salmon waltz elicited bursts of applause, then Ralph beckoned to Tom.

'Now you . . .'

Nervously rubbing his hands against his breeches, Tom sidled on to the ballroom floor. Ralph and Wilhelmina stood on each side of him.

'Just listen to what we sing, and try to do as we do,' Ralph said, in quite a kindly voice. Nervously, Tom nodded. And off they went.

'Push out with your arms – '
'Like that.'
'And flick with your hips – '
'Like that!'
'Then bring up your knees
And then kick with your feet – '
'Like that!'

Tom followed these joint instructions rather well, and was soon beginning to get the idea. He went plummeting across the ballroom floor jubilantly, bellowing, 'I've got it!'

But he hadn't quite. He went too far, too fast, and cannoned into a champagne-carrying coypu, who muttered, 'Oh, yes?'

Tom nervously rejoined the patiently-waiting salmon.

'Try it again, now. Try it again,' said Wilhelmina graciously. And Tom launched himself off once more.

'Make the movements rippling and slow. Don't attempt to hurry,' sang Ralph.

'This is not an underwater show, just relax – don't worry!' sang the champagne-carrying coypu.

And Tom was really beginning to swim now!

'So just glide and then glide again. You'll find it's as nice as pie – ' sang Wilhelmina, and together with her husband added:

'And once you can swim you will really feel as if you're ten feet high!'

Tom was bubbling with happiness and a sense of great achievement.

'I can do it! I can really do it!' he cried.

And all at once *everyone* was swimming and dancing. Rats, minnows, water voles, coypu, salmon, snails, eels – all of them waltzing round and round, with Tom in the middle, swimming as to the manner taught. And this is what the water creatures sang, to give him even greater encouragement:

'In and out of rushes you can go,
Right across an ocean!
You can race or you can take it slow,
Once you've got the notion!

For there's nothing to beat the sport:
It's actually the tops!
As you push with your arms,
And you flick with your hips,
And you bring up your knees,
And you kick with your feet,
LIKE THAT!'

The little orchestra played like a trio possessed, and the music boomed and wailed and strummed and thundered. And Tom was swimming! He was really and truly swimming – to say nothing of the dog Toby.

They had left one young toad, Grout Minimus, on guard at the top of a water-lily. Grout Minimus was far more concerned with watching the glittering spectacle below him than in keeping watch for predators. But suddenly he heard a noise which almost froze him with terror! The sound of three strong killers slipping down the riverbank into the pool! Grout Minimus found his wits. He plunged down towards the glittering chandelier and swung on it crazily.

'Take cover!' screamed Grout Minimus. 'It's the OTTERS!'

44

Five

When Danger Looms . . .

Pandemonium on the ballroom floor one second. The next second – nothing there at all, except an amazed and baffled small boy.

'Get out of here before the otters find you!' yelled one water rat, before disappearing into a tiny hole in the bank.

The three otters saw Ralph and Wilhelmina, and it was salmon they were really after. Two of the otters raced after Tom's new friends. The third, known to his intimates as Ned, was really a little simple, though he was as ferocious as any otter can be when he's balked of a meal.

Ned saw this strange creature standing bewildered, sized him up, and decided that he would probably be good for two square meals or four thin ones. Ned drew himself up, then charged. He was within ten feet of Tom before the boy was aware he was being attacked. Fortunately, Tom's whole upbringing had been based upon survival. Tom moved very fast indeed, and for a short time managed to keep his frantic toes away from Ned's teeth. What a mercy that Tom had well learned the lessons imparted by Ralph and Wilhelmina!

But Tom was a realist. He recognised that Ned was bigger and more powerful than he was, and that, should Tom turn and attempt to defend himself, Ned would unseam him from the nave to the chaps and hang his head upon the battlements. Being no student of the Scottish play by William Shakespeare, the thought that went through Tom's head was: that big fellow'll tear me to pieces and dance on me bones.

At that moment, Toby barked.

Ned halted abruptly. He had heard barking before – but always *above* the surface. He had heard otterhounds after his father and mother – and his father had not survived to dine out on the story. So Ned turned fast, teeth bared ferociously. He saw, not thirty yards off, a small black and white mongrel. Not wasting any time to wonder what a dog was doing underwater, Ned forgot Tom for the moment, and attacked Toby, who allowed the savage fellow to come very close, then darted off towards a silted area where there was a pile of old bottles, dumped from ages long since gone. The dog disappeared amongst them.

Tom, saved with no time to spare by Toby's quick wits, cast about for a hiding place. His eye was caught by an old, overturned fish-basket. Tom swam down to this, lifted it up, and crawled inside.

Ned had at the bottles, snarling terribly. He hurled bottles in all directions – but by now Toby was hiding behind a rotting wooden pillar. In fury, Ned stalked off, brooding on the unfairness of the canine race. His eyes were taken by an overturned fish-basket. Ned sat on top of the basket and began to think. (Slowly, to be sure, but thinking *is* what he was doing.)

Tom realised immediately what had happened. Had he been patient, he would have waited until some idea had struck Ned, and Ned had moved off to translate the idea

46

into physical movement. But Tom was not by nature or training a patient boy. So he raised himself until his shoulders were taking the weight of the basket, and Ned, and began to tiptoe across the pool bottom towards some friendly-looking reeds.

But even Ned, slow Ned, began to think there was something subtly wrong about a fishbasket that carried him from N to M without so much as by your leave, or a small emolument. He moved stealthily off the basket. As stealthily, Tom eased himself until the basket was securely touching bottom.

Then Ned very cautiously raised the side of the basket. Fish swam in and out. Tom saw Ned and Ned saw Tom . . .

Ned hurled the fishbasket away with a roar of rage, and Tom, made a great dive for the nearby pile of bottles in which Toby had earlier found shelter.

For three whole minutes, Ned chased Tom round and round rotting posts, in and out of dense weeds, and through shoals of startled minnows. Tom realised his strength was ebbing. Like it or not, he would have to stand or fight. Hefting an old green bottle – one of ten which an aged pedant had left there a century ago after composing a nursery song about them – he waited for Ned to attack. Ned came at him quickly. Tom dodged behind a post which had formed part of a long-abandoned jetty, then bopped Ned very hard with the bottle.

Instant pain, cartwheels of light, and a giddy sensation all assailed the hungry otter. He felt back on his bottom into the soft mud, and rubbed his head. He could see that Tom, the light of anger in his eye was waiting, bottle raised, to bop him again; and somehow Ned had lost all stomach for this particular confrontation.

'How's a chap supposed to have his dinner when his dinner don't fight fair?' he asked reproachfully.

'Fight fair!' screamed Tom. 'You attacked me before we was even introduced and what sort of game is that, I'd like to know? You want to eat me up, and when I defend myself you say I don't fight fair? Rubbish!'

47

'Now you're insulting me,' Ned complained.

'Fiddlesticks! Also stuff and nonsense!' cried Tom, and gave a few practice swings with the bottle. 'Well,' he snapped. 'Are you going to leave me alone?'

Ned muttered sulkily, 'Who wants a skinny old eft, anyway?'

'I am NOT an eft!'

'Some sort of . . . albino newt?'

'No! I'm Tom, and I belong Up There!' the boy gestured upwards with his green bottle. This information gave Ned food for thought.

'Up There? Then you're a long way from home, cobber.' (Ned had once fallen into conversation with an Australian otter, and had been particularly impressed with his colleague's racy turn of speech.)

Tom was quick to take advantage of Ned's first friendly remark. 'You're a clever, brave sort of otter,' he said cunningly. 'I'm sure you could help me to get back.'

Ned preened himself. 'Well of course, as an amphibian I could certainly get you back . . . But what dangers to live through first, me old China.'

'Dangers?' Tom asked, and his stomach began to flutter a little. He thought he'd had enough of dangers already.

'Otterhounds, old man,' Ned explained. 'Eat you up quick as you like and no questions asked. You're too small to defend yourself and too slow to escape.'

'Then what am I going to do?' Tom howled.

There was a pause, and Ned began to examine Tom in so appraising a fashion that Tom felt obliged to heft the old green bottle once more.

'You can put that down,' said Ned wearily. 'I'm not going to eat you. I've been thinking.' He had.

'What have you been thinking?'

'I reckon that, all in all, the bad with the good, the rough with the smooth, give a little – take a little – you must be one of them Water Babies I've heard tell of.'

'Water Babies?' said Tom excitedly. 'Where?'

'I've never met one,' Ned admitted. 'Not I myself personally speaking. But if you could find them, they'd put you right, wouldn't they?'

Tom began jumping up and down with excitement. 'Oh yes! I'm sure they would. But where would I find them?'

'You'll have to go out to sea.'

Tom had never seen the sea – had hardly ever heard of it, not in the industrial heart of Yorkshire. So he was flummoxed. 'Which way's the sea?'

Ned, appalled by such ignorance, indicated the direction of the sea with one beefy arm.

'Downstream.'

Tom swam across to Toby, who had been listening to the conversation with his head on one side and his ears cocked. He had not, unhappily, been granted by the mysterious lady the gift of understanding the human language, nor of speaking it.

'Come on, Toby. Downstream!' Tom urged him.

'But be careful!' Ned was looking at them, a finger to his lips. 'There's lots of dangers ahead for an innocent little chap like you,' he admitted. 'I'd come with you part of the way, but I'm getting hungry.' And the otter laughed uneasily.

Tom clutched both Toby and the old green bottle.

'So good luck!' With that, Ned swam fast away upstream to rejoin his cobbers.

'Goodbye . . . and thank you!' Tom called.

When Ned had vanished round a bend in the river, Tom addressed himself to Toby. 'Water Babies! Just think, Toby, we'll soon be among friends!' And he and the dog turned, and began to swim strongly downstream.

The tributary in which they had swum for so long now joined the main river, but Tom and Toby were so tired they did not realise this. They swam on and on, and when they were tired, they rested, curled up with Toby snug in Tom's arms. Both lost all count of time, and time was difficult anyway in that strange underwater world of theirs.

Presently, Tom decided to take a chance and see what was happening up above. He carefully broke the surface

of the river and looked about him. What he saw was an enchanted world, but it was the real world also. Up ahead of him was a humpbacked bridge – and over the bridge came trundling a haywain. The land sloped gently down towards the river. To his left was a fine spinney; to his right, ploughed and blooming fields. The sun was quite high, and Tom, lying on his back, floated on the surface, enjoying the peace and warmth. Then something struck him lightly on the nose. He shivered. Something struck his lip, and his chest, and his arms. It was raining! A light rain, certainly, but over there to the east, dark clouds had banked and were steadily advancing. So Tom swam just beneath the surface, then looked up again. The rain struck the water, and a myriad golden showers seemed to spring up where it had fallen. Tom fell into a reverie, in which he imagined the rain, instead of shattering on the surface of the river, fell directly down. He wanted to play among the raindrops and dodge them, as he'd tried to do in broad daylight when coming home from work.

What excellent fun it all was underwater! It was so fine and rare an adventure that Tom simply couldn't help himself making up a little song, which he crooned for his benefit and Toby's. It will never find its way into Mr Palgrave's *Golden Treasury*, but it went like this:

> Oh . . .
> *You can't get wet when you're under water,*
> *Can't get wet when you're in a stream:*
> *Warm as toast, and snug in the rushes:*
> *That's the water-baby's dream!*

The rain it falls on the just and unjust;
On the tip of the Lord Mayor's nose;
On the edge of the serjeant's bay'net;
On the unofficial rose!

But you can't get soaked when you're in the river,
Won't get drenched when you're in the stream;
Warm as milk and smug in the current –
That's the water baby's dream!

This was all very well as long as the rain continued to
fall fairly lightly. But a storm was at hand. Such a storm
as had every old man in the county consulting his calen-
dars and Almanacks to find when such another storm had
been. It was a real howler! Wind fit to uproot every tree
in the area, to lift off every barn door and farmhouse roof.
Even pigs flew! Though the reason is disappointingly
simple. These pigs had escaped from their styes, and gone
foraging across the broad shoulder of Powell's Hill. And
as everyone knows, Powell's Hill is a positive wind-trap.
So the nine pigs were suddenly hit by an alarming boomer
of a wind which swept them off their feet and high over
Balsam's Farm. They landed, squealing and terrified, but
otherwise unharmed, in the cattle-pen belonging to Abram
Lucknow. That worthy, seeing pigs apparently flying on to
his property, at once impounded them. Later, their true
owner, Seth Arblaster, had to take Abram to court before
he could reclaim his Mysterious Flying Pigs.

Meanwhile, this powerful storm was having a considerable effect upon the river in which, only minutes before,
Tom and Toby had been enjoying themselves so much. It
positively churned, and Tom was terrified. He and Toby
attempted to grip reeds, weeds, passing stanchions, anything, in order to slow their increasingly rapid progress
downstream – but to no avail. They passed a powerful old
trout, battling his way upstream, who shrieked at them as
they passed, 'Turn back! Go back! Rapids!'

Impossible advice for Tom and Toby to take. They were
in the grip of currents too powerful for inexperienced

swimmers like themselves to resist. They were being drawn, inexorably, towards the rapids.

In its descent over and through the great rocks that formed the rapids, the river fell over twenty-five feet. This may not seem much on dry land, but when you are being pitched about like a cork – almost dashed to pieces against threatening rocks, or sucked into some vicious little vortex – and when you are rather less than two feet high, then a fall of twenty-five feet, spread over fifty yards, is terrifying. Tom and Toby lost contact with one another the moment they were engulfed by the rapids. Tom felt he was living in a crazy, shifting world. Sometimes he was deep underwater, and sometimes he was actually hurled right out of it. Only his quick wits and wiry frame saved him from being beaten to death against the ugly rocks that studded the centre of the rapids. Bashed, bewildered, deafened, exhausted, terrified, Tom was swept on and down . . . Eventually he lost his senses for a time, and was mercifully unconscious. In his new, relaxed state he was simply carried here and there effortlessly, as though he had been a rag doll. He went with the terrible flow of water wherever it might take him.

When he recovered consciousness, he was drifting idly and placidly. He looked about him. He was about fifteen feet under the surface of the river. What he saw on both sides of the river were old abandoned hulks; rotten, semi-submerged craft, moored forever to decaying jetties, the forgotten relics of an unsuccessful battle against the sea, or poverty. Beneath him, on the muddied bottom, were other wrecks. All this distressed Tom, so he swam on faster, feeling weak, depressed and sick. He wondered what had befallen poor Toby. The dog could have stood no chance in the rapids. His one friend in the world, apart from Ellie, was dead and gone. Tom trod water and sobbed. Sobbing underwater is a curious experience and has to be seen to be believed, and you can never actually *prove* you've been sobbing, since you are surrounded by water which absorbs the tears as soon as they spring to the eyes. Nevertheless, Tom cried miserably. And Toby arrived.

Toby was anxious to explain to Tom what had happened to him, but being unable to speak the lingo of the underwater world, he contented himself with leaping into Tom's arms and trying to wash the boy's face – something else which is a tricky little operation two fathoms down. Tom was overjoyed, but he was also beginning to look rather green about the face.

'I'm not feeling very well, Toby,' he moaned. 'Let's get out of this place as quickly as we can!'

What he did not realise was that he was feeling *seasick*. The change from fresh to salt-water, and the effect of the ebbing tide upon the estuary in which Tom and Toby were now swimming, combined to produce a shock to his system that he could not overcome. He had always lived in the centre of a large inland city – apart from his one excursion to Harthover Hall, of course – and although he had heard about the sea often enough, he had never seen it, let alone been immersed in it.

Had it not been for the comforting presence of Toby, Tom would have broken down completely at this stage of the game. But the dog remained entirely unaffected by his frightening passage through the rapids, and by the transition from fresh to salt water. So long as he was by Tom's side, Toby remained cheerful, inquisitive, and hopeful. Toby it was who led the way out of the harbour-mouth and into the clear waters of the bay. Now, both of them could pause to enjoy the sight and sensation of good clean sand beneath them, and darting shoals of fish flickering about them. At least a day must have passed since Tom made his terrifying plunge into Dead Man's Pool, so it must have been about ten past one in the afternoon, with a scorching sun above, when Tom and Toby encountered their next major problem.

They were swimming close to the sea bed, over slabs of lichened rock, playing in waving sea-wrack, darting past anemones and tall, rubbery clusters of seaweed, when they heard a deep, harsh, angry and undeniably Scottish voice exclaim: 'Confound it! Confound it! Drat my stupid curiosity!'

Six

Enter a Friend – in Need!

On the surface, above Tom, were a number of bobbing glass and cork floats. Depending from one of the floats was a sturdy line. Tom followed this line down and discovered a lobster-pot.

Attached to the outer side of the pot was a big old lobster. One great claw was wedged firmly between the bars of the pot, and the lobster was heaving and straining to free it. He was having no success at all.

'All my own fault! I've swum these waters, lobster and lad, for forty years, and now I'm daft enough to be caught like this!' And he heaved away once more at his trapped claw.

Tom and Toby hove into his line of vision. The lobster, far from showing pleasure or even interest, snapped, 'What do *you* want, young feller, hnh? Hnh? Speak up, now!'

Alarmed, Tom backed off a little.

'I was just wondering . . .' he said nervously, 'why you were holding on to that thing.'

The big lobster, as far as his limited freedom permitted, fairly danced with rage.

'Holding on? Holding on! The wretched thing's holding *me*!'

At that moment, a strange plunging noise distracted all three. They saw, to their dismay, that another lobster-pot, not twenty yards from them, was being hauled upwards rapidly. In it was an eighteen-year-old lobster named Tim. He was inestimably sad, as well he might be, poor fellow.

'They've got me, Jock! They've got me!' he wailed plaintively.

Jock looked far from sympathetic. He grunted angrily and rattled at the cage holding his claw in fury.

'There goes another stupid fellow! He'll end up like me, boiled and garnished for the Lord Mayor's banquet!'

Tom and Toby exchanged startled glances. 'You mean, they're going to catch you and *eat* you?' exclaimed Tom.

Once again Jock danced with rage.

'Of course they are, you numbskull! We're the most expensive food on the menu at present, and they've been after me for years!'

Because he had been an underboy, if not an underdog, all his life, Tom was quick to feel sympathy for creatures in a like predicament. Frightened of this formidable Jock he certainly was, but his fear was less than his concern.

'Oh, sir,' he said, 'I wish you'd let me help you.'

Jock turned away; he was secretly touched by this approach, but it went against his nature to show his finer feelings in public. So he answered very gruffly 'Don't talk balderdash, yer thin buffoon! If all *my* strength can't help me, how can *you* do anything, yer skinny jackanapes!'

Crestfallen, Tom looked sadly at his toes. Jock relented a little.

'Och, yer heid's loose but your hairt's in the right place,' he concluded. 'Come here, then . . .' Tom and Toby swam forward eagerly. 'Now d'ye see. Try to pull that bar away from my claw . . . there!'

Both Tom and Jock heaved and twisted. Toby tried to help by taking a fold of cloth at the seat of Tom's trousers between his teeth, and heaved too.

'Ach, it's madness,' said Jock. 'I'm well and truly stuck!'

Then the line attached to the cage began to tremble and shake!

Jock seized Tom's arm with his free pincer.

'Hark, lad!'

They listened. They heard faint booming and splashing noises.

'What is it?' asked Tom fearfully.

'The lobster-catcher's on his way. He'll be hauling me up in a wee minute!'

Jock renewed his efforts to free his claw. Tom helped. They pulled and strained desperately, but the pincer was firmly stuck. Tiring, they had to relax their efforts momentarily. Then the rope twitched, and the cage began to swing a little.

'Face facts. I'm done for,' admitted Jock.

'Oh no!' Tom cried.

The cage began to rise. Not fast, to be sure, but steadily. Tom redoubled his efforts to prise the two terrible bars apart. Never had he worked so hard at anything. But the surface came closer and closer.

Then Jock began to intone the old fighting song of the warriors of his nation.

> 'Scots who hae wi' Wallace bled,
> Scots whom Bruce has often led,
> Welcome to your gory bed –'

He broke off abruptly, for he realised that within seconds they would break the surface.

'Get off the cage, laddie!' he bellowed. 'I won't have you caught as well!'

Tom glanced upwards. The keel of the fishing boat was alarmingly close, and Tom thought he could see the fisherman leaning over, drawing up the remaining feet of rope.

'One last try!' he shouted.

With both hands, Tom gripped the left-hand bar. With both feet he shoved against the right-hand bar. Jock heaved away at his own trapped claw, and roared one astonishing jussive subjunctive:

'Pipeclay up the lum!'

And as the cage broke the surface and the fisherman reached out for it, Jock's claw was suddenly released!

With great shouts of exultation, Tom and Jock and Toby tumbled down and round, hooting and capering. They hit the sea-bed gently, and Jock embraced the happy boy.

'We did it! We did it!' cried Tom. 'We fooled that rotten old fisherman!'

'Not we. *You*,' said Jock soberly. He slowly steadied himself, and adjusted his plaid and his Tam o' Shanter.

'Before we shake on it,' he told Tom, 'I'd be glad to know who just saved ma life?'

Tom grinned shyly. 'Tom's my name – and that's Toby.'

Toby, hearing his name, wagged his tail joyfully.

'Put it there, then, Tom,' said Jock, and held out his recently-liberated claw. 'And a thousand thanks to you, too, Toby,' said the gruff old creature, and patted Toby's head gently. Tom was so overcome with all this that his eyes filled with tears.

'What's this? What's this then?' said Jock loudly. 'Tears, at your age?'

Tom smiled shame-facedly. 'It's just that – I've never saved anyone's life before . . .' he sniffed.

Jock shouted with angry laughter. 'Well, laddie, you have now! The life of the lobster who's known from Lerwick to Milford Haven as *Jock of the Orkneys*!' With this, he clapped Tom so stoutly on the back, that the boy was hurled headlong into the sand.

'Och, it's all such high cockalorum!' Jock bellowed, tweaking his whiskers. Tom stood up, blinking.

'I've heard Mr Grimes and Mr Masterman saying high cockalorum,' he said. 'But I've never understood what it meant.'

'Never knew what High Cockalorum meant?' Jock roared. And surprisingly, burst into instant song.

'High cockalorum means lots o' things tae me:
A Saturday night in Glasgow, wi' a lassie on my knee!
A swirl of the kilt, the magic lilt
Of a Hieland fife and drum!
Och, it's really grand, you understand –
It's pipeclay up the lum!
And wi' friends along tae sing a song,
And drink a wee, wee jorum,
It's Scots wha hae! It's Hogmanay!
It's High Cockalorum!'

After this, they swam on together, until they discovered a convenient buoy where they could rest for a while and chew, as Jock racily put it, the fat.

Tom lost no time in explaining to his new friend what he was trying to do. As soon as he mentioned wishing to visit the Water Babies, Jock removed his Tam o' Shanter and scratched his head thoughtfully.

'The Water Babies, ye say? . . . Aye well, I've heard tell of the same.'

'You have?' Tom shouted. 'Whereabouts?'

'I'm told, on guid authority, that they have a great playground in the Middle Ocean. But!'

'Where's the Middle Ocean?'

'But. It's a long, long way for a wee bittie bairn like yourself to be travelling alone.' Jock sighed raspingly, and began to fill his pipe with sea-tobacco. 'D'ye see,' he said slowly, 'apart from the normal . . . eh . . . hazards . . . of sea-travel, there's an added danger these days. A great killer shark!' Tom blanched, and his eyes fairly popped. 'A monstrous great shark who prowls the great seas of the world, looking for Water Babies tae enslave.'

'But why would he want to capture Water Babies?' Tom asked.

'Why? Ach, he takes 'em off tae his lair – Shark Castle – and sets 'em tae work for him day and night!'

This was extremely bad news for Tom, and he began to bounce up and down in an agitated fashion.

'But unless I find the Water Babies I'll never be able to go back Up There!' he cried. 'I must see Ellie again. I must explain to her that I didn't steal the swag!'

This, of course, meant absolutely nothing to Jock, and and he wasn't greatly interested in Tom's past history, but what did concern him was that the boy who had so gallantly saved his life was now in A State.

'Ye're mad tae want to go Up There. Land creatures are no guid tae any man. But since your hairt is set on finding these wee Babies, ye'll need a reliable guide.' He puffed at his pipe slowly, then added, 'And Jock of the Orkneys is the best guide in the Seven Seas!'

Tom grasped the tough old pincer excitedly.

'You mean – you'll come with us?'

Jock struck off into deeper waters quickly, so that Tom would not be able to see he, Jock, now had tears in his eyes.

'Someone's got to look after you, you young hothead!' he said.

No one is absolutely certain for how long the three friends travelled, but for those of you with a liking for strange places and unusual journeys, I'll briefly tell you the route taken by 'the most reliable and quite the best guide in the Seven Seas'. They swam into the North Sea and headed south. In the Straits of Dover they encountered some indifferent weather, and things were not much better in the English Channel. Once, however, in the North Atlantic, they went deeper, and swam through a very cold dark world indeed. Two hundred miles southwest of the Azores, the most reliable guide in the Seven Seas had to confess – privately, of course – that he was undeniably and horribly lost. So he continued due West, deciding to put in to New

York, where certain of his more reliable friends hung out. But Toby, secretly sensing that poor old Jock was out of his depth, as it were, cunningly took the lead and made due south for a long, long time. Until one day, Jock, searching about for sea-tobacco, made an astonishing statement.

'You realise, I hope, that beneath us lies twenty-four thousand feet of ocean?'

(They were, incidentally, just on the surface, and finding the weather tolerably good for the time of year.)

'Twenty-four thousand feet!' Tom exclaimed. 'That's really very deep indeed. But how can you be so certain?'

Jock adjusted his plaid and said very formally, 'Laddie, we have just entered the Sargasso Sea, and I think ye'll find, if you should ask any navigator worthy of his salt, that this particular sea is twenty-four thousand feet deep!' With that, he submerged on the instant. Lobsters are not keen on pottering about any surface on any ocean – who knows what marauder might find and eat them? Naturally, Tom and Toby followed him down and down and down. Here the water was green and weed-strewn, warm perhaps, but eerie in the extreme. Then Tom found his feet in contact with something firm. He was on the deck of a sunken galleon!

A weird sight met his surprised eyes. For all around, as far as he was able to see through trembling weeds, were the hulks of old sailing ships – a beautiful but corrupt world of decayed privateers, rotting frigates, wrecked barques. Tom swayed a little on the tilting deck, and found he was grasping an old, tarnished bell for support. The bell boomed eerily and dismally. Tom and Toby were very frightened.

'All those fine ships – wrecked!' muttered Tom. Here and there they could see the muzzle of a cannon peering from a port; or a mast, caked with barnacles, swaying slowly in the undercurrents, weeds drooping from it. Occasionally, and more shockingly, they could discern grinning skeletons sprawled against fo'c'sles, or across dark deck-cannon.

Jock joined him on the tilting deck, and, having found his sea-legs, said ponderously, 'Aye, this is the grave of many a tall ship. Buccaneers and privateers, searching for booty on the Spanish Main, and pursuing their prey out here . . . But all of them after the battles seem to have ended up in this grimly graveyard. The Sargasso has them in her grip till Judgment Day!'

'I don't believe I want to hear stories like that,' muttered Tom nervously.

Then all three jumped in terror.

For they had heard an extraordinary sound, apparently issuing from the wrecks around them, like all the muffled mad laughter of the world encompassed in a single echoing horror.

The three friends wheeled and stared, searching fearfully to discover where the appalling noise came from. The echoing, hideous laughter seemed to rebound from masts and capsized keelsons, from yawning gunbarrels and grinning skulls.

Jock managed to find his voice again. 'It's the Haunter!' he groaned. 'Get out of here!' And the last word echoed dismally. 'Here – here – here – here – here!'

With Jock leading the way, the three companions dived from the galleon and swam about fearfully, seeking somewhere to hide from the Haunter of whom Jock had spoken with such evident terror. Tom now outstripped Jock in his determination to find a place in which to hide. He swiftly made his way through the dim green water to the deck of another wrecked galleon, and disappeared down a rotting companionway. Toby and Jock were not slow to follow him. But the dreadful laughter followed also!

Tom swam on until he came to a wardroom. The three friends swam inside, and Jock and Tom managed to secure the heavy and happily intact bolts. Then, panting, they looked about them. What they saw was not reassuring.

Seated at the head of the wardroom table was a skeleton, still covered with remnants of a once-proud uniform. This motionless figure held them speechless; then Tom noticed, to his horror, that the skeleton's right hand was moving very slowly, and the skeletal fingers were tap-tap-tapping on the oak of the table. Even though he was the veriest land-lubber, Tom realised that the skeleton could not possibly be alive, and that the movement of the hand was due to some current – perhaps caused by their own hasty arrival in the room. Nevertheless, the sight and the sound made him desperately uneasy. Had not that mad laughter been booming outside, he would have quit the wardroom and the ship and not stopped swimming until he had left the dreaded Sargasso far behind.

Toby, however, not concerned with the awesome figure at the head of the table, was busy scrabbling at a fine old wooden chest in one corner of the room. It stood about a yard long and a yard high, and once it had been secured by great iron hasps. But centuries of immersion in salt water had rotted wood and iron, and Toby scrabbled to some effect. Intrigued in spite of all his nervousness, Tom crossed to the chest and hurled back the great lid. He gave a gasp of amazement. The chest was full of treasure!

Pieces of eight, doubloons, Louis d'Ors, gold cups, jewels, diamond-encrusted ornamental daggers . . .

'Blimey!' said Tom. 'I'm glad Mr Grimes isn't here to see this, or it wouldn't be here much longer!'

Then the shattering laughter rocked the wardroom, and above them, on the deck, they heard a slow, ominous regular beat, as of some monster slowly making its way across the deck and *towards the companionway*.

'It can't get in here – can it?' quavered Tom.

'Never a chance, fine mannie!' cried Jock. But he was too terrified to lend conviction to this assurance. The heavy footfall was obviously coming down the companionway and towards the wardroom. Toby, suddenly panic-stricken, hid under the table behind the skeleton's legs. Tom attempted to lift an ancient cutlass which he had found standing against the bulwarks. It was too big and cumbersome, even given its lessened weight under water. In desperation, he rummaged in the treasure-chest and came up with a fine dagger of Toledo steel. It was quite as big to him as a broadsword would be to a man of average height, but he felt comforted. Jock had found a pike, with enough of its handle intact to make it still a formidable weapon. 'Remember, laddie, courage always wins,' he told Tom. But both of them were very scared indeed as the terrible footsteps slowly approached the locked door of the wardroom.

Then the bumping steps ceased. The monster, whatever it was, must be trying the handle of the door. Tom and Jock stood very close together, gripping their weapons. On their faces was an expression of abysmal terror. Outside came a short, vicious burst of chilling laughter. The door began to move. The hinges began to creak. The bolts began to stir. And abruptly the door burst open!

They saw the most grotesque creature they had ever set eyes on in all their remarkable journey. It was a seahorse – but a seahorse of gigantic proportions. And its huge eyes stared at them malevolently, seeming to blaze with an uncanny green light. Tom and Jock dropped their weapons and clung together. Toby tried to vanish between a crack in the floorboards. Time seemed to freeze as the terrible creature gazed at them.

Then it spoke – and they were dumbfounded. Because its voice was mild, light and twangy:

'Frightened you boys, did I?'

A few minutes later, all four were lounging around on the foredeck of the ship. The seahorse was in tears.

'Thirty-five years I've been patrolling these wrecks – thirty-five years! And you're the first people I've had the chance to terrify. The relief, I promise you!' His shoulders shook, and the embarrassed friends could see that he was dabbing at his eyes with a very large, very white, very lacy kerchief. Tom wanted to re-assure him.

'We really were very frightened,' he said.

The seahorse's face became more animated.

'Were you really? Oh, how kind of you to say so. But what are you all doing here?'

'We're looking for the Water Babies, so they can tell me how to get back Up There. I'm a land creature, really,

and I'm far bigger than I seem to be, so I must get back. There's a friend of mine, a girl called Ellie, who probably thinks I'm a thief and I have to get back to tell her to stop worrying and then there's Mr Grimes.'

This story was very garbled, and most of it can have made no sense whatsoever to the seahorse. But he was enchanted by it.

'My dear, what a charming and *romantic* story. But you have a long way to go yet if you're looking for the Water Babies.'

Jock – the finest guide in the Seven Seas, came strutting down the steps from the poop-deck where he had been sulking a bit, and swaggered across to them like the old sea-dog he generally was.

'Ach, it's no sae far, I'll be bound,' he grunted. 'We'll just continue due East –'

'Due West,' said Tom.

'Due South,' said the seahorse.

'And we'll be there,' concluded Jock, exactly as if the

Masterman, Grimes and Tom gazed in awe
at Harthover Hall...

"Faster," yelled Mr. Grimes after Tom.

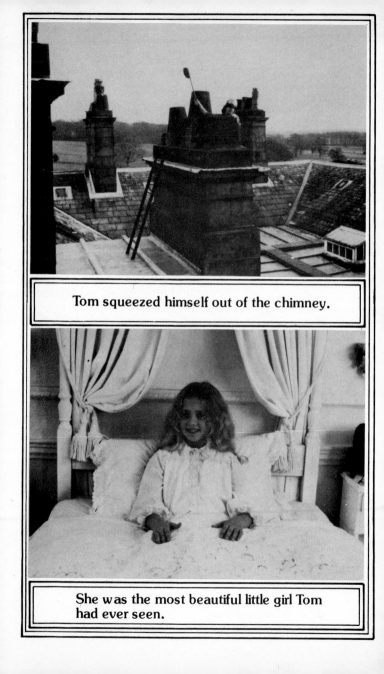

Tom squeezed himself out of the chimney.

She was the most beautiful little girl Tom had ever seen.

Tom stood at the very edge of Dead Man's
Pool, ready to jump...

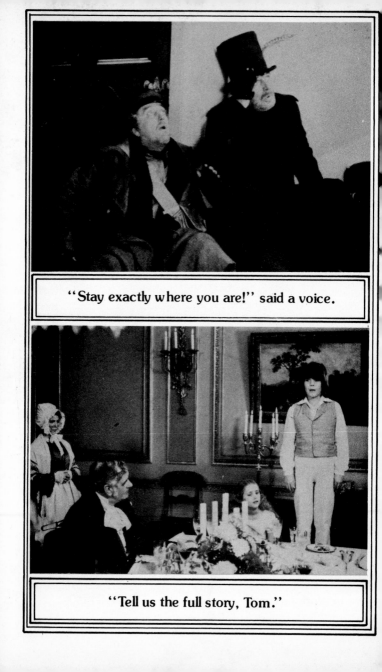

"Stay exactly where you are!" said a voice.

"Tell us the full story, Tom."

other two had not uttered a word. Then he turned to the seahorse. 'What d'ye mean, due South!'

The seahorse's face grew melancholy again. 'It's from the South that I hear the Babies singing sometimes, when I'm lonely. And I'm often lonely . . .'

Tom led Jock off quietly a few paces and muttered something to the gnarled old lobster. Jock nodded vigorously, puffed at his pipe, then both returned to the seahorse.

'Do you think you could lead us there?' Tom asked. 'To where the Water Babies are?'

The seahorse looked at him with hopeful and brilliant eyes. 'Well, I could *try*.'

'Of course you could,' boomed Jock.

'And I wouldn't be a nuisance to you?' said the seahorse.

'Of course you wouldn't!' they both reassured him.

'Then I'd love to come with you! Oh, I can't tell you how wonderful . . . it is . . . to have . . . friends!' And here the poor chap once again began to sob, and blew his long and rather unusual nose elegantly.

'Cheer up, man!' bawled Jock. 'Pipeclay up the lum!'

'Oh, what a lovely name!' said the seahorse, rather obscurely. 'And you can call me Terence.'

'Well, I'm Jock, this is Tom, and the wee mongrel goes by the name o' Toby. So here's our hand on it, man, and high cockalorum to one and all!'

'High cockalorum?' said Terence. 'My dear, I can't tell you how far that takes me back!' And he began to sing. The odd thing is that he sang to the same tune that Jock had sung for Tom shortly after his release from the lobster-pot. From the relish with which Terence sang, it became rapidly obvious to Tom and Jock that the poor fellow had been far too long away from his beloved Thames.

Terence, proud, pleased, and deliriously happy, sang:

High Cockalorum: it really says it all –
It's diamonds and tiaras, it's the Royal Albert Hall!

It's a musical play that's terribly gay;
It's High Society!
It's looking your best, being beautifully dressed –
It's going out to tea!
In the end it's having friends –
Oh, I really do adore 'em!
It's heavenly! It's ecstasy! It's High Cockalorum!

Then Jock and Tom joined in the chorus, and Toby danced about in time with their rhythm.

It was just as well that they could not foresee the future. Because it held for them perils the like of which none of them, apparently fear-hardened by now, had ever imagined, even in his most distressing nightmares.

Seven
Some Terrors of the Deep

We must now think back for a few minutes to the beginning of the fearful chase across the moors. You will recall that once Grimes had seen Ellie galloping after her uncle, he was in fear that she would tell Sir John who the real silver-thief had been. Mr Grimes was perfectly right to dread this, and, according to his own lights, it was very intelligent of himself and Mr Masterman to sneak away quickly before the Squire of Harthover turned the hue and cry on *them*.

They abandoned Wilfred, as being too slow and too conspicuous, and made across country as fast as possible.

They did not dare return to the city to pick up what meagre belongings they possessed, in case Sir John had already sent riders in to inform the local police of what had passed at Harthover Hall. Should this happen, as it shortly must, then officers of the law would most certainly be waiting at Mr Grimes's and Mr Masterman's lodgings against their return. So the two abominable scoundrels decided that the only way they could safely outwit the police would be to find some obscure fishing village, where they might steal a small boat and sail down and round and up the Thames to London, where, in that teeming city, they would be safe from prying eyes. With a little careful poaching on the way, they did manage to reach a small port. Mr Masterman investigated cautiously all one day, and that night, just after half-past eleven, when the moon was a ghostly glimmer and the tide was full, both men crept into a small craft and stealthily rowed out of the harbour and into the North Sea.

Neither gentleman was entirely used to hard work, and an hour's rowing exhausted them mightily, so they were glad, once they had crossed the bar, to hoist sail and let the wind do the work for them. But neither gentleman was entirely used to sailing a small craft in the North Sea. In

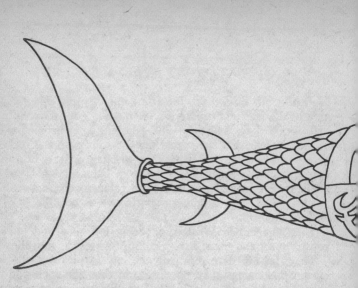

fact, they had never been afloat in their lives before, if the truth be told. So, having fixed the rudder in what seemed to them a southern direction, both men fell asleep.

They woke to find rain lashing them, and soon they were in the mother and father of a storm. Too frightened to move, they hung on to the gunwales for their lives, and watched great winds rip their sails to shreds. The waves began to pound them brutally, and at last one huge column of water lifted them very high into the air, overturned the craft, and dropped it carelessly back into the sea once more. Mr Grimes and Mr Masterman were as frightened of the water as Tom had been. They, too, fell and fell and fell, then for a time lost consciousness.

When Mr Grimes awoke he was in warm seas and moving. He felt he was moving powerfully and gracefully, and he couldn't understand why, since he was certain he must be dead long ago. Then, to his terror, he saw a long, sinister electric eel pouring through the water towards him.

'Here, be off with you, you great beast!' Mr Grimes quavered fearfully. The eel quivered and tingled.

'Would you say that again, please?'

'You what?' gasped Mr Grimes.

'Would you say what you just said again, please,' said the eel. And there was something oddly familiar, to Grimes's ears, about his voice.

'You what!' he said, failing to grasp what the eel really wanted him to say.

The eel came closer. 'Crikey!' it said at length. 'I could've sworn that was my poor old friend Saul Grimes's voice! Him as is long since dead and drowned in the cruel North Sea!'

'My stars!' croaked Mr Grimes. 'Can that be thee, Damiel Masterman? I thowt thee dead and drowned for sartin sure!'

'*Are* you Saul Grimes?' said the eel.

'Of course I'm Grimes, you madman!'

The eel flickered away, and said in a hollow voice, 'How you've changed, Saul! How you've entirely changed!'

'How dost tha mean, Masterman! It's thee as is changed!'

'Saul, Saul. You're no longer the companion of my middle-age; no longer the fellow as used to sit with me in *The Hangman's Rest* and sup your gin whilst I enjoyed me beer. Saul Grimes, you're a fifteen-foot shark with teeth like I never seen in all me puff!'

'A shark!' roared Grimes.

'A shark,' said the eel.

'And dost know what thou art?'

'I'm Damiel Masterman,' said the eel confidently.

'Tha'rt changed entirely, Damiel. Tha'rt a girt long, slithery, crackly, venomous type of eel, and tha gives off blue lights all vicious and constant!'

The eel tried to examine itself, and eventually caught sight of its own curling tail. 'My oath, Saul, you're right!' he said. 'By the stars, old mate o' mine, what've we done to be translated into horrifying brute beasts like an eel and a shark?'

Mr Grimes – the shark – thrust forward vigorously, and his great rapacious mouth was terrible to behold.

'This – is all the fault o' that spoilt young brat, me apprentice Thomas! He's the one as turned the tables on me back at Harthover! And if I ever catch sight of him, I'll tear the living flesh from his body, strip be strip!'

'Fat chance of that, Mr Grimes,' said the eel. 'If you and me is doomed to roam the great waters of the universal world and young Tom is living brilliant in Yorkshire!'

So Grimes (the shark) and Masterman (the eel) roamed south in search of ever warmer waters. And because a great shark and an electric eel can travel much faster underwater than can a very small boy, a tiny dog, and an ageing lobster, Grimes and Masterman were soon scavenging not far from the Eternal Playground of the Water Babies. And when they actually caught sight of the Water Babies, Grimes conceived a plan!

Once upon a time he had lived moderately well, for Tom did all the hard work for him and received nothing in return. And if he could live moderately well on the efforts of *one* small boy . . . how well might he not live on the efforts of dozens of small boys – and girls!

Time to return now to much more delightful people – to the four companions: Tom, Toby, Jock and Terence, the amiable seahorse. Terence had navigated quite well until they crossed the Tropic of Capricorn, then he, too, had become hopelessly lost. The waters in which they were presently moving were unusually shallow and hot, and great weeds grew from the sandy bottom of the ocean. As they swam further, the weeds grew thicker, until after a time the friends realised they were moving through an enormous and evil-looking submarine forest. This depressed them a great deal, and Tom, though fearful of hurting Terence's feelings, nevertheless felt obliged to ask, 'Are you sure we're heading in the right direction?'

'I'm certain of it!' said Terence, with far more assurance than he felt.

'Hnph!' grunted Jock. 'Then we must keep our eyes wide open for the Killer Shark, my mannies, for they say he roams hereabouts in search of food and slaves!'

But though all kept their eyes wide open, none thought to look *upwards*. Otherwise, they would have observed with no pleasure at all that they were being shadowed by an enormous killer shark and a horrendous electric eel!

'It can't be possible!' Grimes the shark was saying. 'I can't believe evidence of me own two peepers!'

'Young Tom transmogrified?' exclaimed Masterman. 'And isn't that his whelp, Toby?'

The shark and the eel circled round one another, fairly crowing with surprise and delight.

'Of all the wide ways of the world for him to travel,' purred shark Grimes, 'young Thomas had to choose this spot to cross my path!'

By now the four friends were deeply entangled in the sinister underwater forest. These saltwater trees had gnarled and vicious parodies of human faces, and their lower branches and twigs looked too much like arms and hands for Tom's comfort; whilst their semi-exposed roots appeared as bizarre, tentacle-like feet. Tom hurried on, and in doing so stepped over a fallen stump. As his rear foot left it, the stump raised itself slightly, and its eyes

71

blazed with hatred. Then a strange, discordant, low humming began.

The friends were in a small clearing. but, as they looked about them, they saw to their horror that the narrow path through which they had arrived was now enclosed, and that wherever they looked, there was no possibility of getting out. They were encompassed by these gnarled horrors – and the terrible trees were slowly advancing on them. The humming increased.

'What was that?' squeaked Tom.

'Don't think I care for this place very much,' Terence said, peering about nervously.

'It was you who brought us here, my fine mannie!' Jock reminded him.

Trying to ignore the fact that the forest was fast encroaching on them, Tom tried to move forward, but there was virtually no way through the malicious, humming, devious undergrowth in which dark and ancient eyes blinked and peered at them.

'We'll have to go in single file,' said Tom. Terence, who was terrified almost senseless by now, and had no intention of being last in the file. streamed ahead of Jock and Toby and tucked in behind Tom. saying, 'I'll, em . . . I'll just stay right here behind you, Tom – and, erm . . . guard your back!'

Jock and Toby. no whit less frightened, tightened up their file, and the four friends, pressing close one behind another, tried to move on. But a great branched arm swung round, seized Tom round the waist, and yanked him up and away from his companions. Tom yelled and struggled, but within seconds the branch had set him down in the thickest of thickets – and his limbs were entwined by supple, mouldering branches and strong roots. The more the boy attempted to free himself, the faster he was held by the evil denizens of the underwater forest.

His friends had been treated in exactly the same way. All were now trapped, separated by several yards one from another; all terrified; all struggling. Then they heard a perfectly foul and ringing laugh . . . They looked up.

A great shark was surging towards them, teeth bared in a hideous grinning rictus. Beside the shark poured a vast electric eel, crackling and spitting, and giving off sinister blue sparks. The four companions were by now quite unable to move with terror. Shark Grimes swept up close to them.

'No need to fear, my beauties! I shan't eat you yet, Mbwahahahah!' (Have you noticed that real villains, the deep-dyed scoundrels of this world, always make the sound of Mbwahahahah! when they laugh at their victims' misfortunes?)

'You shall remain prisoners here,' Shark Grimes continued, 'until we have the entire Water Baby kingdom in chains, then we shall drive you all off to Shark Castle! Mbwahahah!' He flicked his great tail and swung off up and away from the terrible forest.

Eel Masterman flickered down very close to the abject Tom, sparks issuing from his vile mouth.

'Keep away from me!' shouted Tom, manfully.

But Masterman giggled and lisped, 'I could destroy you now – with one flick of my tail . . . but I shall reserve that pleasure for a later date. Meantime, you shan't escape – my eye No! Our friends of the forest will hold you fast!' And Masterman flickered away after Grimes, leaving a trail of malicious sparks behind him.

Terence was sobbing with fear amid his foliage. Since the most deadly enemies had gone, if only temporarily, Jock summoned up his courage with a considerable Orkney effort.

'Pull yourself together, Terence!' he snarled.

Toby was trying to bite his way out of his trap and reach Tom. The boy continued struggling.

'What does the shark mean to do?' he called to Jock.

'I warned you of him, didn't I?' the lobster reminded him. 'He needs more slaves for that castle of his. And we and the Water Babies will have to do his bidding!'

'We shall have to get out of here, Jock, or I'll never see Ellie again!'

For some reason, the last words echoed and re-echoed.

73

'Never see Ellie again . . . see Ellie again . . . Ellie . . . Ellie
. . . Ellie . . . !'

Who knows how these things occur? At the moment when
Tom gave out his desperate and despairing cry, Ellie was
out riding in the massive grounds of Harthover Hall,
accompanied by the keeper, Mr Sladd. Though the day
had started brightly enough, it had become, very suddenly,
overcast and menacing. Ellie and Mr Sladd were walking
their horses after a good exhilarating gallop, and Ellie was
lost in her thoughts. Normally, there is nothing pleasanter
than to sit on a horse and let it walk along, while your
mind – free of the need to control the fine animal if it has
been well schooled – can range over a multitude of topics.

But Ellie was in no mood that day for observing the
beauty of the country around her. She was entirely pre-
occupied with thoughts of Tom. After the dreadful moment
when he and Toby had plunged into Dead Man's Pool she
had almost run amok. Her distress had not been lessened

by Sladd's discovery, half an hour later, of a filthy, tattered, sodden and sooty little jacket. Yet Sir John and Mr Sladd were puzzled. The fact was that many sad people over the years had chosen to leap into that mysterious pool when earthly troubles became too much for them. What tended to happen was that their bodies disappeared for perhaps three or four days, then the corpse would appear, usually half a mile so from the pool itself. But no sign of Tom had been granted to the many estate workers who joined in the search up and down the river. And the boy had been gone for weeks now. With heavy heart, Sir John confided to Lady Harriet that the poor lad must have been caught up in weeds or reeds at the noxious bottom of the pool, and been held there forever.

But Ellie, nonetheless, had the persuasion that somewhere Tom was alive, and thinking of her as often and as deeply as she thought of him. And on that particular moment on that specific morning, with clouds suddenly lowering over the moors and a harsh wind rising, Ellie felt undeniably close to Tom. She halted her horse and stared unseeingly at a great stand of sycamores. And faintly, from their quiet depths, she thought she could faintly hear the little sweep's voice calling: 'Ellie again ... Ellie ... Ellie ... Ellie ...!' And the girl knew a sensation similar to the one Tom had felt when first he had seen the 'bodiless lady' in the booth – and the old hag on the heath – and Mrs Tripp – and the veiled and black-robed lady by the pool. Sixth sense, thought-transference, empathy – call it what you will.

'Miss Ellie! Miss Ellie! You feeling all right, Miss Ellie?'

Mr Sladd's words cut across Ellie's thoughts. She started like one awakened from a long sleepwalk.

'Oh, Mr Sladd, I – ' And she shivered violently.

Mr Sladd rode across to her, his face worried. 'Why bless you, Missie, you're catching a chill, you are.'

'No!' Ellie cried emphatically. 'I felt just now that Tom is alive, and is trying to call out to me!'

Mr Sladd felt as deeply about the boy's tragic disappearance as did Ellie, or Sir John, or Lady Harriet, or anyone on the estate. He felt his presence by the pool, far from distracting Tom, had been the major factor in causing the boy to jump. His own heart ached as he tried, as tactfully as he might, to talk her out of this black depression.

'How can he be calling you, Miss? We've searched the county for miles around – we've dragged the river from the pool to the rapids – but we ain't seen no trace of that boy since he jumped into the pool!'

'He's alive! I know he is!'

Sladd shook his great head. 'If he was alive we'd have found him, and you know it. Don't go giving yourself more grief by thinking a miracle can happen. Aint good for yer peace of mind.'

Ellie's horse tossed his head and snorted nervously. Ellie absently patted his neck as she said, 'Miracles *can* happen! They must happen! Wherever he is, and whatever he's doing, I know that Tom is thinking of me, and trying to come back to me!' And the sad, determined little girl urged her horse into a canter. Sladd was taken by surprise.

'Miss Ellie! Not so fast now! That there Ringwood he's a girt powerful hanimal!'

But Ellie was galloping on, and her long fair hair blazed behind her like the trail of a comet. The heavy Sladd used his hand hard on his horse's flank, and thundered after her. The clouds were rising and clearing, and sunlight fell across the meadows, illuminating girl and man as they moved fast over country that had changed not one whit in recorded history.

How strange then, that when, half an hour later, Ellie and Mr Sladd came trotting into the stableyard, black clouds had once again amassed. As Ellie dismounted, there came a crack of thunder, and Ringwood reared, rolling his eyes till the whites showed. Great Sladd's arm reached for the reins and controlled him. Normally, it was Ellie's pleasure to remove his tack and lead him back to the stall, where Dickon would rub him down. But today, in her strange mood, Ellie did not even bother to thank Mr Sladd for accompanying her on that day's ride, when he had little enough time to spare for his own six children. Instead, white-faced and odd, she strode off out of the yard and into the rear entrance of the Hall.

In the downstairs cloakroom, she eased off her boots, and gave them, with her hat and gloves and crop to Nell, her maid. Nell sensitive to the little girl's moods, did not attempt to distract her with jokes or kitchen gossip, and Ellie walked across the great reception hall and up the wide, curving staircase. There was another crack of thunder. Rain began to fall very heavily.

Ellie washed and changed, and stood alone in her beautiful white bedroom. Mrs Tripp had long since personally supervised the cleaning of every speck of soot that Tom had brought into the room as a result of his misadventures in the chimney. Ellie, looking at the spotless carpet, found herself longing for just one grimy footprint to remind her that her first conversation with Tom had not been a dream.

The rain beat against the windows. Outside, trees tossed their branches against the side of the house. Ellie walked across and looked out over the dark, tempestuous world beyond. Her heart ached to think of where Tom might be, what he might be suffering, and all because the grown-ups had been too hasty to listen to her explanation. Was Tom hungry, or thirsty? Where would he shelter in this drenching pour? Would he ever be able to rejoice again in the delight of his youth, and speed, and the bright spirit that had made him human when so much about him had been dirty and degrading?

'Miss Ellie?'

Ellie swung round, startled. Mrs Tripp was at the door, peering over her round, gold-framed spectacles.

'Try not to worry, dearest,' the housekeeper gently advised her. 'Tom's alive, and he's thinking of you.'

'Oh, Mrs Tripp!' sobbed Ellie, and ran to those comforting arms. Mrs Tripp stroked her hair and soothed her and made quiet crooning noises.

'Shall I ever see him again?' pleaded the girl.

'You will. Be very sure of that.'

Eight
Five Against the Ocean

Tom, Toby, Terence and Jock were still struggling against the great trees of the submerged forest. Since they could not escape, and since they had nothing to lose, they began singing songs to keep their spirits up. Toby could only try to wag his tail, as he was unable to sing a note. Jock had exhausted his lengthy repertoire of Scots ballads and Glaswegian catches. Terence, whose tastes were more erudite, had contributed Gems From The Opera, but now, he, too, fell silent. Tom kept them going with a number of songs of doubtful provenance which he had heard in *The Hangman's Rest*. He gave them a rendering of *The Ballad of the Sweep's Apprentice*, in a particularly high and piercing voice, and then fell silent, racking his brains to think of something new. However, the effects of its delivery were to be far more beneficial than he could ever have imagined, because the song wafted up over the villainous trees, and continued with maximum fidelity to a little clearing perhaps half a mile away, where one or two very interesting things were taking place.

A swordfish was practising sword-play. He was a very fine swordfish indeed, and his name was Claude, pronounced Clode since he was of French extraction. Claude's father had been a great admirer of the works of Alexandre Dumas, and his favourite story was, of course, *The Three Musketeers*. He was a particular admirer of the character of debonair young d'Artagnan. Indeed, when Claude was born, his father announced to his colleagues with pride, 'Now we 'ave a d'Artagnan in the familie!' But his mother absolutely resisted this notion. ' 'Ow can I possibly be calling out "d'Artagnan!" every time I want to feed 'eem and put 'eem to bed?' she demanded. Eventually, mother and father compromised, and the infant swordfish was named Claude d'Artagnan Dumas at a slap-up christening off the Moroccan coast. When Claude grew to early man-

hood, his parents saw to it that he would live up to his
name by subscribing to thirty consecutive copies of *The
Waterproof Gazette*, the journal that is required reading
for any thinking fish. Why only thirty copies, you will ask,
and why consecutive? The answer lies in the fact that the
editors of the *Gazette* decided to bump up their circulation
by serialising popular novels. They first ran *Don Quixote*,
which attracted a large following amongst the squids and
octopus; this was followed by '*Toilers of the Sea*' which
was thought by many to be too near the bone for comfort;
then followed '*Great Expectations*', which the southern
whales read with immense enjoyment – although the sharks
found the yarn greatly over-rated and too full of coin-
cidence for their liking. After that came *The Adventures
of the Three Musketeers*, and it was then that Claude's
father took out his subscription.

Claude now thought, dressed and acted like d'Artagnan.
He had a rakish hat with a long feather, and a superb wig
in the seventeenth-century style. He wore a baldric and

79

scabbard, and a tiny, cheeky cloak. And Claude loved adventures. His sword was the sharpest and best from Tasmania to the mouth of the Amazon, and he was always rescuing virgins and robbing the rich to give to the poor. (Sometimes he thought he was Robin Hood.) The one treat that Nature seemed determined to deny him was a pitched battle with a unicorn. His mother had patiently explained to him that the unicorn is a land animal, and in any event only to be found these days in the remoter areas of Cappadocia, and Claude was a sea-beast. But Claude continued to live in hopes.

The end of Tom's soulful ballad reached his ears as Claude ran through a practice killer-shark. He withdrew the sword from the body – which was, in fact, a carefully shaped piece of rotting timber, and looked about him. His hat-feather bristled with excitement.

'Mais what ees thees? An aventure?' And without ado, Claude raced out of his clearing and sped through the interesting waters towards the deadly forest. Soon he saw four strange figures struggling and yelling to him. Claude, utterly contemptuous of the humming and hideous noises made by the deadly trees when they saw his approach, homed in on Tom.

'What ees the matter, mon gars?'

'We're captured, sir! We need your help!' bellowed Tom, who thought the swordfish a very fine fellow indeed. Claude took a turn or two around the general idea, and familiarised himself with the specific conditions under which Tom, Toby, Terence and Jock were labouring. Then he twirled his moustache and loudly announced:

'Mes amis – fear no more! I, M'sieur Claude, weel deliver you, immediatement!'

He drew back, then plunged down towards Tom, his sword glittering and rotating. In a brace of shakes he had shorn through the branches holding Tom, and he at once turned his attention to the others. The trees, hissing and groaning, moved back before his determined forays. Soon all four friends were free, and in an open clearing. The evil trees closed ranks, and formed a large square round the foursome. There was some grumbling conversation amongst the undergrowth, then two gigantic trees marched forward, side by side, to offer formal combat to Claude.

That lissom chevalier laughed aloud. 'What! You fools! Dare to do battle with Claude le Vite, Victor of a hundred duels?'

Swiftly altering his sword's angle so that it now resembled a bandsaw, he lunged at the two great trees and reduced them to mere kindling in one minute and three seconds flat. Tom, Jock and Terence cheered and yelled.

The trees retreated inside a great wooden stockade. From here they began hurling logs at the adventurers with great brutality and accuracy. The friends dodged about under this heavy shellfire until Claude caught the missiles at swordpoint and hurled them back even faster and more accurately! His shattering fire reduced the stockade in short order, and the trees began retreating in panic. Claude, taking every advantage of their confusion, swooped down on them and ripped them into little atomies. Soon only a score of very discouraged trees could be seen, tottering away and nursing their walking wounded. It had been a complete and most triumphant rout, and the friends cheered Claude to the very echo.

Claude plunged back to them, gave himself a lap of honour, then swept off his fine hat and bowed.

'Was that not magnifique, mes enfants?'

'Magnifique?' they yelled. 'That was high cockalorum!'

Claude threw back his head and began *his* version of a certain song whose broad outlines, you will recall go something like this:

> ' 'Igh Cockalorum is really magnifique!
> It's Camembert, the Croix de Guerre –
> It's kissing on the cheek!
> A French mam'selle who's oh, so belle!
> And a lovely Paris night!
> The flash of steel, that's meant to kill –
> The challenge to a fight!
> With one – and two – and three – and four,

Why wait for any more, um?
Allez! Allez! I lead the way
To High Cockalorum!'

And so a new ally was added to the determined little band. Now all they had to do was to find the Water Babies. Surely, after what they had already gone through, that should be a relatively simple business? Not entirely.

Claude, as the one most likely to know this part of the sea bed, was appointed pathfinder. He made great speed, as you can imagine, and the others found it impossible to keep up with him. So Claude would race off to look for dangers, then speed back again to rejoin them; just as a young dog out with his master will cover twenty times the amount of ground that the man does, with his endless racings and sorties, and hunting for bones, and challenges to other dogs, and stealing tennis balls, and chasing the wind occasionally. But Claude loved action, even it wasn't necessary. He felt that merely by dashing about he was accomplishing something. All in all, he was a most captivating and inspiriting addition to the group, and none of them could fail to love his zest, his beauty, and his infectious high spirits.

They came at length to a great mountain under the sea, and from the peak of this they looked down, one sunlit evening, upon an enchanted world. Far below them lay a great plateau, from which reared broad craters. All was rock and lichen here, and the colour was a pale amber. It held peace, and space, and a little of the magnitude of eternity. For a long time the friends stared at this majestic spectacle, then slowly they swam down from the peak towards the great plain. Here brilliant fish darted and turned, and two mermaids gave them 'Good Evening!' in sweet mellow voices. They were, Tom was glad to see, otherwise occupied in combing their long yellow hair and admiring the effect in handsome oval, coral-framed looking-glasses. Jock was rather nervous, however, as he had been brought up on the Border Ballads, in which all mermaids are potentially dangerous, and some were known to have enslaved and murdered young clerks who fell in love with them.

Just then, Claude came darting back to them, with a certain anxiety in his eyes.

'Do you theenk we find the Water Babies before Shark does?'

'We have to!' Tom shouted. 'We must warn them of the dreadful danger they're in!'

'Aye. And they also have to tell ye how tae get back Up There,' Jock reminded him.

At this, Claude shook his fine head sorrowfully, and fell in beside Tom.

'I don't know why you want to be a land-creature again, Tum.' (That was how Claude used to pronounce Tom's name.) 'There ees far more excitement down 'ere.'

'That's all very well,' the boy replied. 'But there are certain people Up There who think I did something awful, and I must go back and tell them what really happened.'

Although this was a bit obscure, Claude brightened immeasurably.

'Ah well, that is different! When a man's honneur is at stake, he must clear 'is name, at whatever the cost!'

Terence, meanwhile, had been scouting ahead. He felt much braver now in this clean and open seascape, and didn't mind in the least being on his own for one and a half minutes at a time. He scooted back to them, his amazing face crinkled with worry.

'I'm sorry, dears,' he said, 'but I think we're going the wrong way.'

'Hoots and away wi' ye, man!' roared Jock. 'We're heading due South.'

'East!' cried Claude.

'North!' yelled Terence.

'West,' piped Tom.

A noisy wrangle followed.

Then Tom kicked up and away a little, and put his head on one side. Toby paddled up to him, and cocked his head, too.

'What ees eet?' enquired Claude.

'Sssssh,' said Tom, and put his finger to his lips.

Claude nodded, and tried to do likewise. The others grunted and listened. Could they be hearing aright? Or was that . . . singing from somewhere by or in the crater?

'Do you hear it?' pleaded Tom?

'Here what, young shaver?' grumbled Jock.

'Music!'

They surged round Tom and listened carefully . . . 'No music!' they announced.

'But there is!'

'Och, Tom, you're a tired wee fellow, and –'

'I can hear it, and it's coming from over there!' He pointed towards the crater. A shimmering roseate light was issuing from its mouth: a great radiance. And music. Oh yes, there was music all right.

Breathlessly, the friends slowly swam towards the great melodious crater. Above it, Tom could see to his astonishment and delight, the image of a face. The image was enormous, seeming to smile benevolently on the Eternal Playground within the crater. It was an amalgam of the features of the lady with no body, the poor old hag, Mrs Tripp, and the veiled woman in black. But now serenely, it watched over the activities of the Water Babies.

There were Water Babies everywhere, boys and girls of Tom's age, all singing, darting about, playing, and having an enormously enjoyable time. It became obvious to the friends as they swam down towards the merrymaking that the children all had their own little houses, the size of goblins' country cottages, carved out of the natural rocks. Some of the boys and girls were playing hide-and-seek in and out of these tiny houses, others were sliding down a two hundred foot slippery slope, worn smooth over countless years by Water Babies' bottoms. There were swings and roundabouts and hooplas and coconut shies and every imaginable activity for an outdoor-loving child.

All these activities took place in what were the shallows of the crater. But the water gradually became deeper towards the south end of its length – here, there was a dark tunnel, and the water was an intense Prussian blue. As the

friends swam down, Tom was amazed to find no surprise
at their arrival. The boys and girls smiled and waved to
them as though they were old friends who'd just been out
for a morning's jaunt. Once the group had set foot on the
bottom of the playground, perhaps half a dozen boys and
girls swam over to talk to them. Their chief spokesman
turned out to be a very charming but not over-intelligent
boy called Alfred. His companion, Ariadne, was clearly
the thinker of the set; she had deep blue eyes and blonde
hair and seemed very composed.

'Hallo, Tom!' she called.

Tom was staggered.

'How did you know my name?'

'Water Babies always do know each other's names,' said
Alfred portentously. 'Haven't you discovered that already?'

Tom was taken aback for a moment, then he found
himself saying to the boy, 'You're Alfred!'

The boy nodded soberly. Tom turned to the girl.

'And you're Ariadne!'

Ariadne smiled and pirouetted round him once, saying,
'You see – only a genuine Water Baby can know these
things.'

Tom was greatly impressed. But he recalled at once

the first object of their visit here. 'Do you realise you're all in great danger?' he asked.

Some of the younger Water Babies tittered at this question.

'No danger can come to us here, Tom,' said Alfred. 'This is the Playground of the Water Babies, and nothing can hurt us.'

'Are you sure?'

'Sure!' chorused all the boys and girls.

'But what about the shark?' Tom insisted.

Ariadne placed a reassuring hand on his arm. 'If we stay – *here* – always, nothing can harm us,' she explained.

There was a burst of laughter from nearby. Toby, Terence and Claude were entertaining a large cluster of Water Babies with improvised games. But Tom still felt worried.

'The shark and electric eel almost caught us,' he told her, 'and they swore they would capture all you Water Babies, and take you to Shark Castle to be their slaves.'

'That can never happen,' Alfred told him, quite loftily for a slowish fellow like himself.

'I hope you're right,' Tom replied, doubtfully. 'But there's something else I have to ask you . . . Up There is a girl called Ellie – she looks rather like you, Ariadne.'

'Is she pretty?'

'Oh yes!' Tom said in such heartfelt tones that everyone else laughed.

'Good,' chuckled Ariadne.

'She and I were just becoming friends when . . . something awful happened and I had to run away. I must see Ellie again. Can you help me?'

There was nothing for it now but for Tom to tell Alfred and Ariadne the entire story of all his adventures. They were horrified, and none too hopeful about Tom being able to return to an estate in Yorkshire once he was a Water Baby rather less than two feet long.

'You see,' said Alfred, 'we've heard – and no more, so it may be true or it may be false; it may be a myth, or it may be founded on fact – but there's only One Being who can

decide if a Water Baby may go back Up There, and he is
... the Kraken!'

If a clap of thunder had added weight to this strange
name, the other Babes could not have been more awe-
stricken. A hush fell over the great playground, and even
those boys and girls playing hide-and-seek a long way
away paused in their searching.

'He doesn't sound too friendly,' said Terence, shuddering
a little.

'He's not,' Alfred told him. 'We learn he's very frightening.'

'Frighten-eeng?' roared Claude, and lunged with his
sword. 'Zen I long to meet eem!'

'That's pretty difficult,' said Ariadne. 'He's really a
very important person indeed. The most important person
to all sea-creatures. Because he's the Lord of the Oceans,
and he lives at the Other End of Nowhere.'

'The Other End of Nowhere, lassie?' bawled Jock,
rather rudely. 'Ye're talking through your bonnet. How
can Nowhere have an other end when it hasn't even got
a this end?'

'I'm not absolutely sure that you have any right to talk
to me like that,' said Ariadne calmly. 'You're obviously
something of a traveller, but believe me you've just as
obviously never gone due South of here, or you wouldn't be
quite so uppity about your lack of geographical knowledge!'

Jock was so surprised at being addressed like this, and
by what he would consider to be 'a wee bittie bairn and a
girl-chiel at that,' that Tom could scarcely refrain from
laughter. But he asked tactfully, 'Have any Water Babies
ever gone to find this Kraken?'

A strange blue shadow fell across the little group at this
new mention of the Being's name, and they seemed to
hear a distant and haunting chord, like a gigantic organ,
played in a vast and empty cathedral. Even no-nonsense
Jock felt uneasy, and he decided to let the Babies get on
with their story without further disclaimers from him.
Alfred and Ariadne were looking anxiously at one another.

'Yes,' said Ariadine eventually, and her clear eyes began to cloud. 'Two of our bravest boys – Michael and Peter – decided they'd had enough of living in playtime day in, day out. They could remember what life had once been like Up There, just as you can, Tom. So they set out to find the Kraken, as you want to do.'

'They never came back,' added Alfred, dolefully.

'We heard nothing of their fate,' said Ariadne, and began to weep. Terence, who was readily affected by the misery of others, began to sob also. Claude, touched by this strange tale of heroism blighted, doffed his hat.

'Brave ones,' he murmured.

'They went that way, through the tunnel,' Ariadne told them.

'But it's the only way to reach the Kraken, though,' Alfred added gloomily. The dark tunnel at the far end of the Babies' playground did indeed look sinister. Tom shivered.

'You look exhausted, Tom,' said Alfred. 'All of you do. You must rest first, in my house. Then you can make your plans.'

Within ten minutes, the friends were all asleep. Tom and Toby in a little bedstead with brass rails, Claude on a truckle-bed, Jock asleep in an old rocking-chair, covered with a shawl, and Terence upright, his long eyelashes twitching, propped against the larger bed. Alfred, sometimes a boy of unusual tastes, had found one or two reminders of his days as an earth-child with which to decorate his charming, modernised period cottage. '*Bless this House*,' said a delightful piece of tapestry-work; and above Tom's bed was a remarkable oil-painting of General Wolfe scaling the Heights of Abraham. But in these the friends took no interest. They really were exhausted, and having swallowed a quick bowlful of Underwater Ambrosia, they had turned in. Now they were deeply asleep, and the hour was approaching four in the morning, when human resistance is at its lowest, and the body coldest.

To this tranquil scene Ariadne came rushing in high distress, and begged them all to wake up. She shook Tom and Toby, almost knocked Terence over, and gave old Jock such a start that in angry reaction he almost nipped her pretty little nose off before he realised who she was.

'Quick! Quick!' she was shouting. 'Everybody's gone!'

Grunting and blinking, the friends dragged themselves out of bed and staggered outside, rubbing their eyes disconsolately. The Playground was empty. (You must remember that the Water Babies kept very different hours from our own. They needed very little sleep, and tended to doze lightly almost on the move. Thus at four o'clock of a clear summer's morning you might well expect nearly all of them to be up and about, enjoying themselves and thinking of new games to play and one or two new songs to sing.)

'What happened?' Jock was the first to ask.

'It's terrible!' said Ariadne tremulously. 'You were asleep, and a weird blue light came from the tunnel. All the Babies rushed off to see what it was. I warned them not to! But they took no notice and they all ran inside the tunnel, and when they were all there, the shark and eel trapped them!'

The friends digested this awful news, still groggy with sleep.

'A weird blue light?' Tom said.

'That must have been the eel, luring them on,' observed Jock.

'But they've all gone! Alfred – everyone! What shall we do?'

'Do?' shouted Claude, sweeping on his hat and adjusting his little beard. 'What shall we *do*? We shall rescue them, of course!'

Nine
The Other End of Nowhere

The friends swam south fast, though Tom was very worried. 'I hope we did right, leaving Ariadne alone in the Playground,' he said.

'Man, there was nae other course!' said Jock loudly. 'The Playground is magic and protected, so long as wee idiots don't stray into that dreadful tunnel. But she'd be safe nowhere else. It'll take us all our time tae look after ourselves!'

Claude had other opinions, however. He swept around them, his great sword glinting.

'Hah! Show me the shark who can best Claude le Vite in mortal combat, and I shall show you a dead swordfish!' he cried.

The others realised he made an error of some sort here, but they knew what he was getting at, and they were very pleased that such a resourceful fighter as Claude was with them on this grimly adventure.

They travelled on for several days, wondering how the shark and eel had managed to persuade the Water Babies – who were not accustomed to long hauls under the ocean – to keep up with them. All the time they worried lest the shark might have become impatient with their slowness, or very hungry – and eaten the poor children out of hand, as it were.

At length they reached a great precipice. They looked out and down. Here the ocean floor shelved tremendously, and they knew they were once again looking at some of the sea's deepest waters. A fitting place, they concluded, for the lair of the cruellest shark in the world. Somewhere down and beyond lay Shark Castle, in those demon-haunted waters. And somehow they would have to reach the Castle, and free the Babies. Even Claude was unusually silent for a while, as these uncomfortable thoughts crossed their minds. Eventually, the brave chevalier plunged off the edge of the precipice with that great shout of all true Burgundian crossbowmen, 'Courage, mes enfants! Le diable est mort!'

As I expect you know perfectly well, this means: 'Courage, my children! The devil is dead!' As Tom swam off after the resourceful swordfish, he wasn't absolutely sure if this inspiriting comment was actually true. Terence was missing his skeletons and rotting gunwales, and wished himself far off in the warm green waters of the Sargasso Sea. But now he could do no other than to follow the rest; because of all things in life, poor Terence was most afraid of being alone and friendless. In any case, though he could not be described as the bravest of seahorses, he had a great heart, and had no desire to think of the Water Babies pent in durance vile in Shark Castle. So he quickly scudded past Tom, crying out in quavering tones, 'High cockalorum, Tom!'

All day and much of the evening they swam, until they were approaching a terrifying fang of rock that reared up from the ocean bed. Strange storms played about this ghastly pinnacle, and turbulent eddies threatened to drive the friends away from the menace ahead. But Claude, who could smell adventure a league off, urged them on with many a Gascon and Burgundian oath. As they approached the rocky outcrops of the savage fang, Claude led them up and up for some five hundred feet, until they were able to see exactly what lay at the top of this absolutely fearful natural monument.

'It's Shark Castle!' all the friends exclaimed at once.

The monstrosity – for no other word does justice to it – was perched high on the fang of rock, and backlit by sulphurous glows. The building was constructed from the giant bones of great whales, and from sea-masonry culled from the Dead Sea thousands of years earlier by roaming sharks. It was decorated, too, and was, all in all, a vulgar, eccentric, frightening mixture of porphyry, amber, whalebone and mediaeval masonry. From its dreadful depths came sounds of sinister loutish merriment.

The friends carefully swam up to one of the castle's

four black towers, and, taking care that no one saw them, they peered down at the courtyard below. Torches were burning, suits of shark armour stood in niches and coigns, and tattered shark banners drooped below windows. In the centre of the courtyard an enormous and ribald banquet was in progress, at which the sharks, like robber barons, sat feasting. Shark Grimes and the Eel Masterman were sitting at the head of the table, drinking bumpers of wine and feasting off obnoxious scraps of food served to them by the enslaved and terrified Water Babies.

All the Babies wore convicts' uniforms – grey background with black arrows painted all over them. Sharp-eyed Terence even saw that on Alfred's uniform, the words 'Property of HM Government' were written. To ensure that the captives could not run far or fast, they were weighted down with enormous leg-irons, and they were being treated abominably by all the robber sharks. The friends saw one poor Baby, kneeling by Grimes with a heavy tray of goodies. Grimes selected one and popped it into his mouth, then sent the child spinning with a cruel flick of his tail.

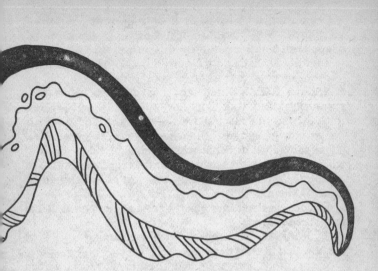

At this, Claude's anger knew no bounds. 'Thees ees . . . assez!' he cried. 'Mes amis, prepare to attack!'

The furious swordfish rose high above the tower and pointed his great sword in the direction of the bestial banqueting table. But Jock and Tom swam up and seized him.

'Stop!' they whispered earnestly.

'Pourquoi?' Claude demanded.

'There's far too many o' them, laddie,' snarled Jock. 'They'd tear us tae pieces in ten seconds!'

Terence shuddered with fear.

'And then the Water Babies would lose their only hope of rescue,' Tom added.

Claude freed himself angrily, and took a swift turn round the tower, his tail flicking impatiently.

'Eh bien! What do you propose, Tum!'

'We . . . we must find the Kraken!' said Tom. Claude frowned, whipped off his hat and wig, and scratched his head in puzzlement.

'The bairn's right, Claude,' Jock assured him. 'This Kraken pairson is our only hope.'

Claude hurled his hat to the floor of the tower. 'Kraken!' he snorted. 'Me – I want to fight those . . . salauds below! Those great bloated, out-of-condition sharks!'

Tom put his hand on the quivering swordfish's shoulder. 'No one doubts your skill or your courage, Claude,' he said. 'And I know you'd take a lot of them before they eventually killed you. But they *would* kill you! There's thirty or forty of them at least down there, and goodness knows how many more on guard that we can't see! We'll come back and do battle with them, I promise you. But when we do, we shall have powerful reinforcements. I'm certain the Kraken won't allow this sort of thing to go on in his Domain.'

Terence was weeping quietly now, as he looked at the ugly scene below.

'Poor Alfred,' he sobbed. 'Such a charming boy! And see how that beast is treating him!'

'Come away, Terence,' said Jock harshly, and guided the sad creature away from the immediate dangers of the Castle.

South, deeper south they swam, and the waters became clear, and blue, and icy cold. They looked up and saw vast icebergs moving infinitely slowly above them, and they were glad that their long journey had acclimatised them to this terrible temperature. It was Jock who first noticed that they were eventually swimming beneath a great ice-cap far in the frozen South, and the friends began to realise that if they did not find the way to reach the Kraken they might be doomed forever to swim about in this echoing cathedral of ice, because now they were almost beneath the South Pole they had lost all sense of direction.

'This must be it!' said Tom.

'Yes,' Terence shivered.

'The Other End of Nowhere,' said Jock, dourly.

Their voices rang hollowly. Claude pointed upwards with his sword.

'Voila!'

Above them, the thick crystal ceiling was delicately traced with frosty patterns, and strange, unimaginable sighings and ringings filled their ears. Tensely they moved along, until Tom found a small, circular hole in the ice. The tingling sounds intensified. Terence swore he could hear sounds as of a monstrous, heavy, obese creature breathing slowly and with a certain difficulty. Tom touched the strange aperture. 'I wonder . . .' he said. 'Is this the way to the Domain of the Kraken?'

The strange tingling musical sounds increased in volume. Then there came a blur of light so intense that all the friends had to shield their eyes against it. When they dared to open their eyes again, the powerful light had resolved itself into a shape. The shape of a beautiful, shimmering, crystal ladder, the bottom rungs of which projected below the hole Tom had found.

'Look at yon!' Jock breathed.

They clustered around the hole and gazed upward. The ladder seemed to stretch forever.

'Come on, zen!' cried Claude, and moved forwards to ascend the ladder. But Tom restrained him, though with difficulty, since Claude was a strong and impetuous fellow, as you will have gathered.

'Claude, you can't! None of you can! Above this ceiling is AIR!' Bewildered, the others looked at him. 'You can't live in air! Only Toby and I can do that. So he and I will have to go it alone.' Toby, tail wagging, sprang into his arms. 'But we'll be back,' Tom promised them. 'With help!'

The others thought this difficult proposition over for a few moments in absolute silence. Then Jock replied, 'You're right, laddie. But we'll be waiting hereabouts. So take care.'

'We'll be here,' whimpered Terence, 'counting the minutes.'

Wordlessly, because he was very close to tears, Tom embraced Jock, Terence and Claude in turn. Then, with Toby under one arm, he set his feet to the bottom rung of the ladder and began to mount it. Hardly had his heels vanished above the aperture than the ladder itself began to move upwards at amazing speed – something close to twenty-nine feet per second, if you are fond of accurate detail. Frightened on Tom's account, Claude and Jock moved forward in a vain attempt to follow him. But the crystal-edged aperture closed – with a thud.

Tom and Toby flew upwards, hair streaming. in a blur of icewalls and speed and blue light and tinkling crystals. Because of the speed of their movement. Tom was in effect pinioned to the ladder. Toby was very frightened, and with his ears set back close to his head he nuzzled into Tom's shirt and prayed for their dazzling ascent to end, very quickly.

Then Tom found his feet were touching, not the ladder, but a narrow crevice of ice. He was clearly in the open air, and the strange tingling sounds were louder than ever. Opposite him was a large tunnel in the immense icewall. Tom nervously set Toby down, and looked without pleasure at the intimidating cavity ahead. Above him were great peaks and crags of ice, with snow driving across them. Winds howled and thundered.

Tom realised that he could never hope to climb up those terrible faces of ice, and assumed that the only way to reach the Kraken would be to enter this vast and forbidding tunnel. Unfortunately, Tom was unable to read, because otherwise he would have realised that the strange glowing shapes above and around the mouth of the tunnel held all manner of negative advice, such as: *'No Admission! Trespassers will be persecuted! Défence de cracher! Hawkers and canvassers please go North! Raucher verboten! Back in time for Childermass! Who's afraid of Archie, then? Remember Carthage!'* Tom looked at all these and he pondered them, but not for very long since they meant absolutely nothing to him. Then he called to Toby and stepped into the tunnel.

The pair of them had covered scarcely ten yards when they were met by a high and buffeting wind. This wind screamed at them. It almost tore the thick hair from Tom's scalp; it almost flayed Toby. It set up icicles in the boy's hair, on his eyebrows and eyelashes, and even in his nostrils.

It filmed his lips until they were frozen together. It crept in fine webs of rimed ice between his fingers and toes. Within a further twenty-two yards it reduced Tom and Toby to ice-covered beings who, heads down and spirits low, trudged on against the blast . . . until a deep harsh voice thundered something incomprehensible at them. Both Tom and Toby stopped at once. The wind reduced its force, and icicles began to fall from their bodies. The freezing hairs on Tom's head began to rise in terror. There came another harsh bellow.

Round a corner, advancing towards them very fast, came a colossal polar bear, rearing up so that his great forepaws were twenty-six feet in the air. Tom and Toby quailed.

Here you are going to point out what every schoolgirl knows – namely, that polar bears are in fact North Polar Bears, and are not to be found in the Southern or Antarctic regions. Nevertheless, here was this great white bear, undeniably a Polar, towering above Tom and Toby. What lessened his awesome appearance a little was that he wore on the back of his head a red-and-white-striped Shetland cap with a red pompom, and round his great neck, and hanging some way down his shoulders, was a scarf of the same pattern. But his eyes, brown-and-gold-flecked, looked merciless, and his voice was savage.

'How *dare* you!'

Tom looked up at this rearing monster and croaked, 'Oh sir, please . . .'

'HOW DARE YOU!'

The bear leaned forward – a terrifying sight – and snatched Tom up with one great paw. Toby whimpered and scampered about the rear paws of the beast. Tom found himself staring into those merciless eyes.

'Out with you, my lad! Trespassers will be petrified!'

With Tom in one paw, the Bear marched off down the tunnel, and back towards the entrance. But Tom was cross now – he had come so far and he would *not* be browbeaten, even by a creature twelve times his size and fifty times his strength. The boy began to shout and kick and struggle.

'I've come to see the Kraken! Do you hear, you bully! I demand to see the Kraken!'

The bear coughed unexpectedly, then began to roar with laughter. (Here I intend to stop calling him the Bear and give him his proper name, which was, of course, Archie.) Archie set down the boy and held his sides as he laughed and laughed.

'What's the matter now!' yelled Tom indignantly.

'Demand, is it?' boomed Archie. 'Well, if *I* didn't terrify you, perhaps you might just amuse His Lordship. Come on.'

So, taking Tom's hand, he led him back up the tunnel, where they were met by a very relieved Toby, and they proceeded on and on and up and up. Then, when a faint seabreeze reached their nostrils, Archie paused, and looking down at Tom, said quite gently, 'Here you are, then. You have now entered the Domain of the Kraken.'

Tom looked out. They were standing on the edge of yet another great ice cliff, but this time they were inside a wall of mountain ice. Far down was a huge, half-frozen sea.

Across it the wind hurled long slanting lines of powdered snow. In the part of the sea which was not frozen, sealions, seals and walrus lolloped and played. Nearer, penguins, looking and acting very much like self-important butlers, dashed hither and thither, carrying trays which contained letters from Muscovy, gifts from the Lord of Crim-Tartary, spices from Aleppo, tiger-balm from Singapore, exceedingly hot peppers from Trincomalee, an unusual wine from the Celebes, and three hundred and thirty-seven partridges without their pear-trees.

When Tom had gazed his fill, Archie, still holding the boy's hand firmly, indicated that they should walk up the narrow ledge that climbed up and up the side of the icy mountain. Tom and Toby felt that at last they really were approaching the strange and clearly powerful being who ruled such vast and forbidding territories. The boy became very nervous. This was much worse, he reflected, than waiting to climb up your first chimbley, or to steal your first mutton pie, or to climb over Farmer Greenleaf's wall and eat his apples when his missus wasn't looking. Oh yes, this was infinitely worse!

At that moment, a song came into Tom's head, and, to cheer himself up, he began to sing it. This is roughly how it went:

Now for the Lord of the Sea!
What sort of thing will he be?
A tyrant or a charmer? Industrious or slow?
A knight in burnished armour? A drama in snow?
Does he appal and astound?
Does he knock small boys around?
I wish I knew the answer: I wouldn't be so shy,
Oh what will Kraken be like – to I?

To his surprise, the penguins answered him.

The Kraken is a creature of no specific mood;
He may decide to eat yer to season his food.
He may decide to greet yer with sticks and with stones;
He may play tunes on your bones!

The albatrosses, wheeling and lunging around the pin-nacles of ice, added:

The Kraken is a master of every known disguise:
We think he will aghast yer when you behold his size!
No tempest or disaster could equal his rage:
Perchance you'll dance in his cage!

How encouraging could they be? wondered Tom as he sought for a new verse.

Will he expect me to stay –
Live life the Krakenly way?
If I were to refuse him, deny him on the spot,
Would this approach bemuse him, amuse him – or what?
Are there no practical wiles
To turn all his tantrums to smiles?
I'd love to know the answer; for this I'd bend the knee:
Oh, what will Kraken be like – to me?

At this point Archie softened, perhaps because at last Tom had got his grammar right.

The best things and the worst things you'd ever want
*   to do:*
That's what the Kraken will be – to you.

And all the other creatures echoed him softly, as the snow fell and the winds moaned and the tiny boy and the tiny dog and the great big polar bear trudged up the difficult track to mystery and tension.

The best things and the worst things you'd ever want
*   to do:*
That's what the Kraken will be to you.

After three hours' of uncomfortable climbing, the strange and ill-assorted trio reached a large crevice. By it, and on a small stool borrowed from St Pancras Station, sat a very large, bespectacled walrus, who was deeply engaged in attempting to solve three down and four across in a tricky crossword puzzle which appeared every third Thursday in the Antarctic edition of *The Waterproof*

Gazette. The walrus, whose name was Cyril, tweaked his moustaches absently. He was very warm in his crevice, and there was always a pot of tea gently simmering on a stove borrowed from the Borrowdale Foresters' Lending Library and Watch Committee Assembly Rooms. He looked at Archie, Tom and Toby without much interest and asked:

'What's black and white and read all over?'

Archie frowned. 'That's a facer, that is, Cyril,' he murmured and scratched his nose.

'A newspaper is!' Tom yelled, because to him this riddle was old hat.

Cyril grudgingly thought it through, nodded, and wrote it down. He didn't want to ask the answer to the last clue, because if Tom got it right, Cyril would have nothing to do until the next edition of the *Gazette* appeared.

'Well now,' he said eventually. 'What can I do for you?'

'This young shaver wants to see the Kraken,' said Archie.

'Put his name on the Waiting List,' said Cyril. Tom and Archie looked about them. Soon they discovered a yellowing square of parchment affixed to the wall. At the top it said: WAITING LIST. And someone, almost certainly Cyril, had underlined it twice, in case anyone did not understand the first time around.

'But there can't be a Waiting List,' said Archie. 'Nobody's waiting at all.'

Cyril looked across at Tom.

'He is.'

Archie and Tom looked at one another.

'How long will I have to wait?' said Tom after a while.

'Till I say you can go!'

'How long will that be?'

'When I've made up my mind.'

'When will you make up your mind?' asked Tom.

'When I say you can GO!'

The ice cubicle by the crevice opened at once, and Tom and Toby jumped inside. Outwitted, Cyril leaped to his feet shouting, 'Come back, you scoundrel!'

But the ice-cubicle, an interesting form of Polar lift, had closed up and vanished in a puff of mist.

'Fair's fair, Cyril,' laughed Archie. 'He out-thought you that time!'

Ten
The Kraken—and After

Up and up shot the strange ice cubicle, and Tom and Toby, huddled together inside, seemed to hear the Music of the Spheres as they ascended at roughly seventy-nine yards per second per minute. Then all motion stopped. The doors opened.

Tom and Toby stepped outside. The doors closed and the ice cubicle descended. They were alone, in the Domain of the Kraken.

Before them was nothing but darkness and mist, stretching much farther than their eyes could see. Thunder rumbled, and brilliant lightning played across this sinister wilderness. A high, thin, wordless wailing began, the sort of wailing that makes the heart knock at the ribs. Then Tom noticed in the great distance a dim light approaching. It was turning, and now and again flickered, almost like a distant glow-worm, though Tom had never been privileged to see a glow-worm. As it drew ever nearer, Tom could just perceive a massive complex of spheres. The outer one was quite still; inside it were six others, of decreasingly small size, which rotated constantly; and the innermost sphere of all, over which were depicted the features of the known world, was dead still.

The great globe came to a halt, suspended in darkness, with mists now and again wreathing it, and lightning playing across it. It must have been a hundred yards away from Tom, and as far as he could judge in the awesome and indifferent light surrounding him, it must also have been two hundred yards in diameter. Tim's eyes started with fear, and he hugged Toby close. But he was a plucky fellow, and decided to take a chance.

'Is anyone there . . . ?'

Only echoes, weirdly distorted, answered him.

'Is anyone there?'

Mist poured from the top of the globe. Thunder rolled

and lightning flickered. Then the mists slowly began to part. And Tom saw the Kraken.

He was sitting on top of the globe, and he was a truly gigantic and terrible figure. Huge, muscular, clad in frozen furs and a great dark cape, with icicles intertwined in its fur, the Kraken was well-bearded, and his hair was frosted. He wore a primitive, powerful crown of ice, in which danced hard blue and silver lights. His face was pallid and his expression ruthless, weary and omniscient. He appeared like a man who had had too much power too long, and was weary with what the exercise of that power might do for him. Vapours constantly drifted between him and Tom. He spoke, at last. The voice was deep, harsh, but compelling.

'Some call me Neptune, Father of the Oceans. Some know me as Poseidon– the Thunderer, the Earthshaker. And some know me as the Kraken.'

Tom bowed his head in awe.

'My name is Tom, sir. Just . . . Tom. And this is Toby.'

The Kraken sighed, and the sound was as of a bleak wind slicing across a frozen continent.

'What do you want with me?'

This was the moment Tom had adventured for. He drew in a deep breath, patted Toby, and began:

'My friends the Water Babies are trapped in Shark Castle. Would you please free them, and let me go back Up There?'

'Boy,' said the Kraken. 'I will give you ONE wish only. That is all I shall grant. If it is good, then all will be well with you. If it is less than good, you will remain forever a captive in my realm.'

Tom shuddered. And he realised just how accurate the information given him by Archie and the other Sea Creatures had been.

'The best things and the worst things you'd ever want to do:
That's what the Kraken will be – to you!

But what could the Kraken mean by good and less than

good wishes? And what about remaining forever a captive here, in this appalling place?

'I'll try. sir,' he whispered.

The Kraken's face relaxed slightly, with a deep creaking of ice.

'I've been watching you for a long time now. You've had many adventures and you've come a long way to see me. So whilst you make up your mind about your wish, please accept the hospitality of the Other End of Nowhere.'

The mists parted between the Kraken and Tom, revealing a long slender spine of rock. Down this track came strutting two dapper penguins, carrying trays with goodies on them. The penguins reached Tom and Toby and made awkward little bows. The first penguin spoke first, as befitted his number in the pecking order.

'For the young gentleman, a thick slice of Dundee cake imported from London regardless of expense by our Mr Nicely of Fortnum and Mason – and a cup of fresh, piping-hot Darjeeling tea.'

Tom was delighted, and thanked the first penguin warmly.

'And for your companion,' the second penguin said – and Toby wagged his tail – 'a bowl of hand-picked Westmoreland biscuits, enriched with nourishing plankton gravy!'

As the bowl was set down for him, Toby sniffed it delicately, and cocked his head to one side.

'Eat up! Drink up!' boomed the Kraken. 'Fortify yourselves for the ordeal ahead!'

So as Tom and Toby ate and drank, the first two penguins were joined by many other penguins, who diverted the friends with a jaunty little dance, and some lively songs that were designed specifically to cheer up people who were about the face what was privately known round here as The Ordeal of the Kraken. But what Tom was concentrating on, as he cautiously ate his way through the huge chunk of Dundee cake that the Kraken had so thoughtfully provided, was this: what is a good choice? And what is *less than* good? Clearly, the penguins wanted

him to choose well. It seemed likely that even the Kraken
wished him to choose well. But there were still vast areas
of doubt. What should he do for the best?

At that moment the commanding voice of the Kraken
was heard.

'Thomas! Your time for choice has come!'

Tom looked up. The green-glowing eyes of Poseidon
were regarding him intensely and narrowly. Then three
penguins trotted forward, and beckoned Tom to follow
them. With quailing spirits he obeyed. And faithful Toby
followed him. What the penguins were now showing him
was odd. Three veiled, misty globes, of some kind of
crystal, had appeared at Tom's waist-level. Each was an
exact yard in diameter. The first penguin gestured to the
first globe. Tom peered at it. Mists clambered about inside,
but after a few moments they cleared, and Tom saw, with
fast-beating heart, that inside the globe there was a perfect
image of Ellie in her riding-habit, astride her bay, galloping
across those moors in which Tom had evaded his Harthover pursuers what seemed an age ago!

'Ellie!' said Tom to himself, and he felt his eyes pricking with tears, because he knew he loved this little girl who had showed him so much understanding and goodwill.

'Your choice!' boomed the Kraken.

Tom was bewildered. Everything was happening so fast! The second penguin was indicating the second globe with a saucy flick of his flipper. Tom trotted forwards, and peered into the second globe. And what he saw was this – the ceiling of ice into which Tom had broken, and below it, his faithful, hopeful friends: Jock, Terence and Claude. White-faced they were, and very anxious, as if wondering if Tom had been murdered on his way to the lair of the Kraken. Tom's heart yearned to reassure them.

'Your choice!' the Kraken urged Tom.

Tom was led by the third penguin to the third globe. Into it he peered nervously. What he saw now was the banqueting area of Shark Castle. No sharks were about, but many a shackled Water Baby was there, with fettered ankles, sweeping up the débris of the previous evening's feast and looking intolerably miserable. What struck at Tom's sensibilities was an image of poor old Alfred, gentle creature that he was, being whipped by some bullyboy of Grimes.

'Oh no!' shrieked Tom, and put his hands to his eyes. When he looked into the globe again, the image had vanished in wreaths of mists.

Tom stepped back from the three fateful globes, his heart pounding and his eyes still bedazzled. What on earth was he to do and say? Frankly, he wanted to be back Up There, telling Ellie exactly what had happened at Harthover Hall, and why he had seemed to be the thief. That was what he wanted. And yet, he felt an abiding loyalty to Jock, Terence and Claude, who had so unstintingly given of their devotion and skill to help him to find the Water Babies. How could he let them down? Yet there again, the Water Babies, whose presence he had sought so single-mindedly, were now all in chains, humiliated and bullied by the great shark and eel and all their bandit crew. So what on earth to choose? How to tell the Kraken that he wanted everything, not just one stupid wish?

'Well?' thundered the Kraken. That august presence was towering over him. The time for choice was NOW! Tom buried his face in his hands once again, and thought and thought. Then, almost with a sinking heart, he knew where his responsibilities lay.

'Sir,' he said. 'I should like you to set the Water Babies free.'

Came a distant crack of thunder.

'Are you absolutely sure that is what you most want?' the Kraken asked.

Tom hesitated. Had he done the wrong thing? He looked at his naked toes, wriggling in the snow.

'Please, sir, set them free!'

The Kraken pondered.

'Very well!'

Tom was glad. He had made his choice, difficult though it had been, and now he was to be rewarded. He scampered across to the third globe, and peered into it. What he saw gave him no grounds for rejoicing. Because Alfred and all the other Water Babies were still enslaved. In wretched, miserable anger, feeling he had been betrayed, Tom stamped his foot and turned on the Kraken.

'But they AREN'T free!'

The Kraken looked at him for a long time in sighing silence.

'I am The Lord of The Oceans,' he said eventually. 'But as such I do not personally interfere with what goes on in my kingdom. The natural laws must prevail, or Nature herself would be betrayed. The strong must prey on the weak, and the weak, unless they are resourceful or can camouflage themselves successfully and so keep out of trouble, must go to the wall.'

Tom did not care about all this ambiguity. He had struck a bargain with the Kraken, and now the Kraken was going back on it.

'I came all this way to see you because we knew we couldn't defeat the sharks on our own. You seem to have said that I made the right choice, yet now you're telling me you can't or won't help me! What kind of Lord and Master are you?'

This was remarkably rude, of course, and Tom should have known better. Yet perhaps his youthful indignation at promises withdrawn did the trick. The Kraken smiled once, grimly, then said: 'You, Tom – you and your friends have the bravery and the wits to defeat the shark and eel. Use all your friends. Use everything around you. I shall be watching.'

The mists played again, and the great globe on which the Kraken sat, vanished into icy mists and lightnings. Tom and Toby were alone again, and apparently no better off than they had been before they had ever reached the Kraken.

Eleven
The Raid on Shark Castle

What was remarkable was that, no sooner had the Kraken disappeared, than Tom and Toby found themselves standing by the ice cubicle once more, and looking at the WAITING LIST sign. Of Cyril the walrus there was no immediate evidence, but Archie the polar bear was towering over them anxiously.

'Tom,' Archie said. 'You look unhappy.'

'I am unhappy. How am I to defeat the shark and his gang?'

'That's a tall order,' said Archie.

'Will you help?' Tom asked him.

'I think we'd better talk to Cyril and the rest. Fifteen heads are better than one.'

'But Cyril – why should he help me? He didn't even like me.'

'Oh, that was just his way. He tends to suspect small boys at first blush. But I think you'll find that, when backs are against the wall, Cyril will be your man.'

We now need to return to Shark Castle, where the killer shark and eel still reigned supreme, and the Water Babies were still very much enslaved.

In the banqueting area, most of the servant sharks were sprawled across the table – some under it – and others rested almost motionless by the great fireplace. Guarding the great entrance with its portcullis raised above, two brutish shark guards tried to keep awake by playing cards. Since both were astonishing cheats, nobody was winning. Shark Grimes was very cosy indeed. His master-bedroom was near the top of the tower, and was, of course, circular. (Have you ever pondered the problems of putting mirrors and pictures on a circular wall, or bookcases and wardrobes against one?) Dominating the bedroom was the bed. This had been looted from a sunk schooner, and carried many leagues to Shark Castle. It was a superb brass bed, and the captive Water Babies had to spend many hours keeping it shining. Shark Grimes' head rested upon a feather pillow, and his body was covered by an enormous eiderdown. Picked out in superb needlework was a representation of the Siege of Salamanca, and had you examined the bottom left-hand corner of the eiderdown you would have found stitched into it the information: *A Present From Purley, 1842.*

By the bedside were Shark Grimes' slippers, and a sea-coal fire burned merrily in the charming inglenook. In the bookshelves to the left of the bed was an interesting literary selection. On earth, Saul Grimes could scarcely read, and only read when he needed specific information. But here, as the robber shark, he found he had time to indulge in a little bedside browsing now and again. In the event, he had fallen asleep over volume two of *The Adventures of Peregrine Pickle*. Pride of place in the shelves was given to that never less than informative volume, *My Years With the Bow Street Runners*, by Inspector Millions, now of the detective force and apprehending criminals spectacularly fast.

In the castle turret, Masterman the electric eel lay with his long strong body curled round a flagpole. From time to time he snored gently, and when he did so, his entire body twitched slightly, and faint blue sparks crackled around him.

In the dungeons lay the poor Water Babies, huddled together for warmth. This night, as on every night since their capture, most of them had cried themselves to sleep. Alfred, however, was too miserable to sleep, and he clutched at the metal grille which served for a window, and stared out across at the stone courtyard beyond, which was just about at his eye-level. As you will recall, Alfred was not the brightest of souls, but he had at least given far more attention to notions of escaping from Shark Castle than had his playmates. The great trouble about living as the Water Babies had done for so long – in the eternal play-ground – is that you are never fit for anything but play.

111

And if something else should present itself – work, for example, or some form of challenge – you are disinclined to become involved; it all takes too much effort. This was why the life of a genuine Water Baby did not really appeal to a boy like Tom. He had worked most of his short life; he had been knocked about and had survived in a brutal and uncaring world. He was the only Water Baby with the drive and determination to do something about the frightful mess the others were in.

Michael and Peter, you may remember, had attempted to move out of the Eternal Playground in search of more demanding activities, and had never returned. In fact what had happened to them was that they had made their way to New Zealand, struggled ashore and established a small fishing village in the South Island. I'm glad to say that they thrived, got along famously with the Maoris, and even taught them a few songs, including certain versions of *High Cockalorum*. In turn, they learned much of the Maori's beautiful history, and at this time they were about to publish a learned volume on the subject, having signed a lucrative contract with a representative of the Oxford University Press who happened to be holidaying in their village.

At any rate, here was Alfred, beginning to regret he had never been more enterprising in the Eternal Playground, and wondering if he could persuade twenty of the Babies to hide behind the grille and jump one of the guards when he came to drag them out to work the following morning. Alfred was by now prepared to die rather than undergo this exploitation, but sadly his contemporaries were too afraid to do anything more than obey their captors.

At that moment Alfred heard an appalling screaming sound. Then great missiles came hurtling down into and through the castle walls! The place was being bombarded with enormous stalactites and stalagmites of ice. And cannonballs of ice some twenty feet in diameter were dropping on the castle. Tom, Archie and Cyril were putting their plan into action!

The battlements were cracked, the towers split, and the

great banqueting-area was utterly destroyed. Some missiles clanged against the section of the portcullis that was slightly lowered, and the card-playing guards leapt up and raced inside, amazed and horrified.

In Shark Grimes' bedroom, a stalactite fully twenty-five feet long ripped through his ceiling and hit the floor immediately behind his bed-head. It tore away the floor completely. Just as Grimes, in horror, sat up, a second missile ripped away the rest of the floor. For an infinitesimal fraction of a second, Shark Grimes realised he was sitting up in a bed which had no means of support.

Then the bed fell.

It fell and fell, because the enormous missile had continued its headlong career downwards, ripping through all the other floors that lay between Shark Grimes' bedroom and the cellars far below. The bed remained upright, but fell very fast, and Grimes saw walls racing past him, and wreckage slowly crumbling in on him from all sides. Finally, the bed hit bottom with a reverberating crash. The impact jerked Grimes clean out of bed, and he was hurled across the floor, spinning over and over on rollers of ice, until he fetched up hard against a massive wooden door. His head juddered and he groaned.

The hubbub, the cries of terror from the guards and the thunderous roar of falling masonry, woke the sleeping Water Babies. They joined an excited Alfred at the grille, and crowded round it, cheering wildly at this sensational turn of events.

The turret was shattered by a direct hit, and Eel Masterman, spitting with fear and sparking wildly, beat a slithery retreat for the staircase beyond. He did not know what was going on, but he sensed that the force of the bombardment was weakening the very structure of Shark Castle, and he wanted to be out of it quickly. But by now Shark Grimes had rallied, and was tearing around trying to organise his vassals into some kind of defensive force. Yet the missiles kept coming. And the castle was trembling.

A new element appeared – a fighting force spearheaded by Claude, Jock, Tom and Terence. They made straight

for the courtyard, and whilst Tom and Jock kept some of
the smaller sharks occupied, Claude dashed at the metal
bars of the grille with his sword. Three determined sorties
were enough to snap off the bars. Cheering, the Water
Babies swarmed out into the courtyard. Tom shouted to
them to follow him. Jock fought manfully as further guards
rushed into the courtyard to cut off the escape route; but a
lobster, however valiant, is no match for a couple of
hammer-headed sharks. Claude urged Jock to follow Tom
and the Water Babies, and himself engaged four of the
enemy simultaneously. These were odds that Claude
enjoyed.

Soon Tom and the Babies were swimming high above
the highest tower of Shark Castle, and able to look back.
With sinking heart, Tom realised that the bombardment,
though it had damaged the castle almost beyond repair,
had not succeeded in putting paid to the warrior lord,
Shark Grimes. Tom appreciated that soon even Claude
would be overfaced with too many opponents, and once
Claude retreated, the sharks would be after them, and they

would certainly overtake them within minutes. So, telling the Water Babies to continue on up towards the Domain of the Kraken, he and Jock swam down once more to see how they could finally defeat their foes.

Claude was fighting superbly. He had despatched eight of his opponents already, and was still fighting with brilliance and gaiety. But he was tiring. This much was evident to Tom. He shouted to Claude to try to contain the guards within the castle walls if possible. Claude jauntily raised his hat, and at once attacked the nearest guards. His speed and skill daunted them. Slowly Claude fought them back until all had retreated behind the portcullis entrance.

Tom and Jock made for the room above the portcullis. Jock shouted, 'Are ye mad, laddie? Going in there?'

'If I can somehow lower the portcullis we shall have trapped them all inside for a short time!' he yelled.

'Aye, for a short time, perhaps. But what happens *after* a short time? They'll be out at the top of the towers, and cut us off!'

They had by now entered the portcullis room, and Tom swam across to where the lever that controlled the massive grille was situated.

'Don't argue, Jock, please! Help me to move this lever!'

The friends heaved and shoved. But the lever was very firmly in position. Jock swam to an embrasure and looked down.

'Claude's tiring fast,' he said. 'The puir fellow cannae last much longer.'

Tom was still heaving away at the lever. Then he found a long spar of tough wood, and using this carefully, was able to exert much more pressure on the lever. Just as Claude's strength began to desert him, the lever moved. Tom was hurled across the room as it spun. The great chains rumbled, and the vicious portcullis crashed down, serving as an effective barrier between the shark guards and the now jubilant Claude.

The three friends swam up past the creaking buttresses of the tower, and as they reached the highest turret, Shark Grimes appeared on it, followed by Eel Masterman and several very large guards. Tom's stomach contracted. They had come so far and done so much. And now, with the enemy only forty feet away, all their hopes were confounded. Within seconds, Grimes and his crew would be butchering them. And when they were dead, the same fate would befall the Water Babies. For perhaps three seconds the friends and their enemies stared at one another, all absolutely motionless. Then Tom, Jock and Claude spoke simultaneously.

'This is the last one. Let's make it a good one.' And they prepared to meet their vast and sinister adversaries.

Shark Grimes was poised for the attack, and his cronies were preparing also. Their mouths opened with satanic grins as they thought of how quickly and easily they would destroy these three impudent coxcombs.

Then Cyril's most enormous ice cannonball fell directly on to the turret! The whole structure exploded, and as it did so, the impact of the great missile cracked the entire castle into a million fragments. The friends, in awe, backed off. That vile lair was disintegrating completely. It was shattering and sinking, plunging down into the primordial ooze far below. There was something malign yet magnificent about such universal destruction. The friends watched and watched until the structure finally came to rest on the ocean bed. Not a single survivor flickered up to avenge this annihilation.

Now that it was over, the friends felt limp, unable to rejoice. They were stunned by the magnitude of their own ferocity. Slowly Tom broke away from the hideous spectacle, and began to swim upwards in the wake of the distant Water Babies.

Twelve
An End – and a Beginning

In a great arena, safe in the Kraken's Domain, everyone was jubilant following the utter defeat of the sharks and the destruction of Shark Castle. Everyone was dancing, in particular the bears and the penguins, and as they danced, Tom and his friends were finishing off the great song that first united them.

'High cockalorum! We did it in the end!
It's thanks to every one of you, my very special friends!

To which Jock, Terence and Claude replied, one after another:

'Och, not at all, sure, we had a ball,
A real old Hieland fling!
And I must insist I wouldn't have missed
All this for anything!
It's a victory for decency, for daring and decorum!
It's magnifique, it's fantastique –
It's high cockalorum!'

When the festivities were at their height, there came a great shimmering globe, and in it were partly seen the splendid but daunting features of the Kraken himself.

'Well done, Tom! Well done, all of you!'

This from the Kraken was no mean praise. Tom blushed, and Archie twisted his paws sheepishly.

'You've made your wish come true, Tom,' continued the Kraken. 'The Water Babies are free.' And the Water Babies all cheered and shouted again.

The Kraken allowed them their moment of enthusiasm, then his piercing eyes fixed on Tom once more.

'But now it's time for your secret hope to come true – to go back Up There.'

There were cries from Tom's friends, and they clustered round him.

'You aren't going to leave us now, Tom, are you?' wailed Terence.

'How shall we manage without you, Laddie?' said Jock.

But Claude, with a flourish, swam forward commandingly.

'Our friend 'as to clear 'ees name with Ellie. After all, that is why he made this adventure! We must not be selfish enough to keep him with us now.'

'You're still determined to return, then, Tom?' Jock asked.

Sadly, Tom nodded. Jock tried to be jaunty, though he was feeling very low indeed.

'Well, lad, we'll miss you – all of us will. But ye've left us wi' plenty to do. We shall make it our business tae look after these puir foolish wee Water Babies, and see that no more sharks imprison them.' Solemnly, Terence and Claude nodded.

'It's time to go, Tom,' the Kraken reminded him.

Tom, very close to tears, embraced Claude.

'Goodbye, Claude. I'll never forget your courage – or your marvellous sword.'

Claude dashed a tear from his eye. 'Adieu, Tum,' he said.

Terence and Tom embraced. Terence was weeping freely.

'Goodbye, Terence,' Tom sniffed. 'Thank you for coming with us. At least you'll never be lonely again.' Terence could not trust himself to speak.

Tom walked across to Jock, who shyly proffered his tough old pincer

'Goodbye, old friend,' Tom said. 'As long as I live I'll never forget Jock of the Orkneys.'

Jock fought hard for self-control.

'Och, away with ye, laddie. And remember the old war-cry – *pipe-clay up the lum!*'

Terence muttered to Archie, 'He's always saying that. But what exactly does it mean?'

Archie scratched his great head, and whispered, 'I think it means keep your chimneys clean!'

Where once the Kraken had been, a glowing globe stood open. It was evidently meant for Tom and Toby to enter. Nervously, and very sadly, they stepped inside, then turned to wave again to all their friends – to Jock and Terence, Claude and Archie, to gruff old Cyril, to Alfred, Ariadne and all the Water Babies. Then the globe sealed, and suddenly it was moving fast, up and up and away from the Other End of Nowhere in a blur of golden light . . .

It was night in the grounds of Harthover Hall. The great lake stood quiet. The birds were still. No breeze ruffled the surface. Then a glow appeared from its depths, reached the surface, and gleamed brilliantly for a split-second, and was gone. In its place stood Tom and Toby, quite dry, on the surface of the lake. Tom, with Toby in his arms, had reached the bank before he realised the nature of the miracle that had occurred. And he realised other things as well. He *felt* rather than *knew* that he was again the size he had been before he jumped into the terrible pool. That he was dirty again, and dressed in the same old sweep's clothes. That Toby was his own proper size again, and as grubby as if neither of them had ever been in water in their lives.

The vastness of the events from which Tom had just emerged seemed distant and small to the boy now – he could not have told you why. Perhaps it was the dislocating experience of travelling at almost the speed of light for some minutes – for how else can you move from the Antarctic to North Yorkshire in no time at all? In any event, Tom was now thinking of nothing but of reaching Harthover Hall. First he wanted to be absolutely sure that Ellie was aware that he had not been pinching the Squire's silver; second, he wanted to convince the Squire himself. Quite how he was going to achieve this he had no firm idea, but his submarine adventures had taught him the value of bold and decisive action, however wrong-headed it might turn out to be. So he gritted his teeth and made for the distant Hall.

It looked near – very near. But fog abruptly intervened, and somehow Tom began to lose his way. He found himself stumbling through night and fog with absolutely no idea where he was. He wiped the moisture from his face and eyelids, and groped his way onwards. Presently he began to smell something interesting – woodsmoke – and something delicious and gamey. He found he was very hungry indeed. Then, piercing the gloom, a few intermittent sparks flared briefly in the air. Tom advanced rapidly, falling down twice before he was within five yards of what appeared to be, on first examination, a derelict cottage. But from the chimney Tom had seen sparks flying, and, after all, he was a chimney-sweep, and who should know about such matters half so well as he?

But it was dark, dismal, and threatening. Tom dared not enter the building for fear of stumbling upon something very unpleasant indeed. Yet he was hungry and he was cold and he was lost.

'Hallo-oh?' he quavered. 'Anyone around?'

A great hand appeared from nowhere and muffled his mouth, and another great hand yanked him off his feet, and an all-too-familiar voice muttered gruffly, 'Someone *is* around, little gallows-bait!'

Saul Grimes dragged Tom inside the building. It was very derelict. An open fire crackled merrily on stones in the centre, and the smoke and sparks were finding their way up a chimney. It was altogether very weird. Loosely tied to a hasp in one wall was Wilfred. Squatting on the floor was Mr Masterman, looking as dank as ever, and leaning forward to turn a rabbit which was roasting on a spit over the fire. Despite his predicament, Tom could feel his mouth swimming with saliva. He was terribly hungry!

'Who would have thought to see this wretch again, Damiel?' chuckled Mr Grimes.

120

'Not I, Saul, not I,' Mr Masterman replied.

Tom suddenly broke away from Mr Grimes's grip and shouted, 'Why aren't you two hanged!'

To his surprise, Mr Grimes chuckled appreciatively. 'You've got plenty of punch and go, Tom,' he said, and squatted down by the fire. 'But I'll soon bring you to heel again. Soon enough!'

Tom made a rush for the doorway, but Mr Masterman seized him and dragged him back. Mr Grimes looked at the defiant grubby boy, and thought a while. Mr Grimes cannot have been such a bad psychologist, because he slowly tore off a juicy hind leg of the roast rabbit and held it up. Tom looked at it, fascinated and famished. Mr Grimes slapped it into Tom's palm and said, 'Just get that down yer, lad, and listen to Saul Grimes . . .'

Mr Grimes' thinking was good. Tom's hunger overcame everything else. He bit and sucked at the delicious meat and bones, and washed them down with brackish tea. Mr Masterman and Mr Grimes were also hungry, and there was other game to cook and eat. Silence reigned for some time, then Grimes reached for his green bottle of gin, and took a comforting draught before passing it to Mr Masterman. Tom looked across at his old master, seeing him through drifting smoke and dancing motes of ash.

'It's Providence that sent you here tonight, Tom,' said Grimes carefully. 'For we mean to clean out Harthover Hall good and proper!'

'You daren't!' said Tom, staggered. 'Not after what happened last time!'

'Ahah, but they think it was *you*, lad. And if you're going to be troublesome . . .' And he mimed the ghastly neck-snapping procedure. Tom shuddered.

'So just pay attention,' Mr Grimes continued, and took another fortifying drink of neat gin. 'After one try, they'll not be expectin' another – stands to reason! So this time we'll clean up the lot and be off and away to London, where no one'll ever find us.'

Tom was certainly listening, but evidently his expression contained something in it that made Mr Grimes add, and this time sincerely, 'You'll get yer share, boy. Saul Grimes was never mean.'

Toby crept across the hovel and laid his head in Tom's lap. The fire was warm. Mr Grimes allowed Tom a good draught of gin, the heat of which, if not the taste, Tom relished. His head began to swim. He was desperately tired, and pleasantly full, and, for perhaps the hundredth time in his short life, very drunk indeed. To think of escaping was all too much of an effort. His head nodded.

'Best move away from the fire, Tom,' said Mr Masterman civilly enough. 'We can't have you singeing your toes, now can we?'

Tom crawled across towards Wilfred and curled up on a half-opened bale of straw. Toby snuggled in beside him. Wilfred looked down at the soon-sleeping pair benignly, his eyes gentle behind their superb lashes. The fire continued to crackle merrily enough, and Mr Grimes and Mr Masterman were content to suck at odd juicy bones, smoke their clay pipes, and take turns at the gin bottle. It was, veritably, a thieves' kitchen; yet for the first time Mr Grimes and Mr Masterman were tacitly acknowledging Tom to be, not a poor whipped creature, but an equal in their forthcoming freebooting expedition. Both of them had sensed in Tom a new spirit of independence.

Neither they nor Tom really credited what had happened to them all for a month or more under the ocean, because that is not the way this kind of submarine magic works. But it is only fitting that a brief account should be given of how Mr Grimes and Mr Masterman came to be translated once more from killer shark and electric eel to their old, familiar and unscrupulous mortal selves.

Following the utter destruction of Shark Castle, Shark Grimes and Eel Masterman were cast up to the surface of the sea in a stunned condition. When they came to, they were clinging to a torn spar, and looking at one another in utter amazement, for here they were sweep and criminal once again, with only the haziest recollection of what had befallen them since they had set out from the English coast in their light craft. They knew they were cold, and dazed, and very uncomfortable, but as to where they were and why, they had absolutely no notion. They were seen by the crew of a collier and taken aboard. Within hours they were in Robin Hood's Bay, still puzzled, but thankful to be alive. Within hours, they had conceived their desperate robbery plan, and set off for the grounds of Harthover Hall.

Now that the agile Tom was with them again, they felt they could relax. They had no doubts whatsoever about the success of the following morning's burglary, and already they were spending the proceeds of their looting in their minds.

In the cold, uncertain light of pre-dawn, the two men, with Tom and Toby, glided over the wet grass to Harthover Hall. Mr Grimes had already selected a suitable place of entry in his mind, and now they were here. Tom shivered violently in the cold, raw mist. He had not had enough sleep, and he had had far too much gin. He was not really himself, if the truth be told. Mr Masterman held Toby firmly under one arm, and tried to huddle deeper into his tattered military greatcoat. Mr Grimes was already issuing instructions to Tom.

'Up that drainpipe to the window over there – because it's open! Now don't look so daft, lad, you'll manage it. Then creep downstairs quiet as a church mouse and let us in by this side door. Now do yer understand what I'm on about?'

Tom nodded, his mind raging. It was all becoming clear to him now, and any sense of camaraderie that the previous evening's eating and drinking might have awoken in his breast was now gone forever. These men meant to use him as the spearhead of a hugely dangerous exercise in robbery, and he knew quite as well as they did what the penalty for such a crime could be. Since he was a boy they would probably not hang him, but he would certainly be flogged and sent off to Botany Bay for ten years or more. Tom was not absolutely sure where Botany Bay was, but he certainly didn't want to go there in chains.

Mr Masterman sensed something of what was going on

in the boy's mind. 'Don't think of giving any warnings, Tom,' he grated. 'For I've got your pup here, and if you cross us, I'll break his little neck, quick as you like!'

Tom knew he meant it.

Mr Grimes gave Tom a leg up, and the boy gripped the drainpipe and shinned up it without a look below. He reached the window Mr Grimes had indicated earlier. It was indeed open a little. Tom needed some skill to force it open further, as it had clearly not been fully opened for years, and all the paint had dried and fixed it in its present position. But he managed, with little noise, to heave it up sufficiently for his slight and nimble body to slip inside. Unfortunately, in landing, his legs hit a meal trolley and sent it scudding across the floor to the door, which it struck noisily. Tom choked with fear and suspense. Someone surely must have heard that awful din? He waited for perhaps a minute then, fearing for Toby's life, stealthily tiptoed over to the door, opened it, and peered out at the landing beyond. Silence, darkness and terror. Yet Tom recollected enough of the geography of the Hall to be able to slip down the great staircase and to work his way into the servants' quarters and to the door by which he and Mr Grimes had previously been admitted by the formidable Mrs Tripp.

It must be admitted that when it came to grand larceny, Mr Masterman and Mr Grimes were scoundrels to be proud of. With speed, stealth and admirable discernment they went through the entire house – including bedrooms occupied by slumbering inhabitants – and soon filled three large sootsacks with booty that would bring them at least two thousand pounds apiece if sold to the right dealer – a Mr Clatworthy of Rotherhithe. And two thousand pounds then would be worth at least twenty thousand pounds now. So that it was with high hearts that Mr Masterman and Mr Grimes, laden with their swag, tiptoed cautiously down the great sweeping staircase. Tom lagged behind . . .

Once inside the house, once realising that these bounders were desecrating Ellie's home with their foul antics, Tom's previously waning spirits received a boost. He knew he

124

could not allow the robbers to get away with it. Tom was not concerned with absolutes like Honesty and Dishonesty, Truth and Falsehood, Virtue and Vice – how could he be? No one had ever taught him these things. From the moment he was able to run he had been a petty thief himself, stealing food, handkerchieves, wallets if he could – anything – to help him to survive in that harsh world he and Mr Grimes moved through daily. Had he been fortunate enough to have been born the son of a belted Earl, there is no doubt that by now Tom would have been a perfect little gentleman. But Tom's upbringing had led his character into entirely different areas. First and foremost – until he met the pup Toby – he had been concerned only with himself and his own welfare. Had he not fought and lied and stolen and cheated he would have been dead years before. His surprise encounter with Ellie had given a new dimension to his life and ambitions. As he stood at the head of the staircase and looked down at the rapidly-descending burglars, he was not concerned that they had stolen; he was concerned about *from whom* they had stolen. And as he looked down at the burglars and across at a suit of armour, he realised that no more options were open to him.

Tom wrenched the suit of armour from its plinth, and, with a piercing cry of, 'Pipeclay up the lum!' he hurled the armour down the stairs.

The clatter would certainly have awoken the sheeted dead had they been by to hear it! Mr Grimes and Mr Masterman never knew what had hit them. Amidst a noise like ten percussion bands rolled into one, they fell and tumbled to the bottom of the stairs.

Then a stentorian command.

'Stay *exactly* where you are!'

Tom looked up. Sir John Harthover, in nightgown and nightcap, was levelling a formidable shotgun at the villains. Next to him was Lady Harriet, leaning over the balustrade.

'Stay *exactly* where you are!' she commanded.

'But, dearest, I've just said that,' Sir John remarked.

Without taking her eyes from Mr Grimes and Mr Masterman for an instant, his lady wife replied, 'So have I, dearest. Say it again!'

Sir John, advancing the position of his shotgun a little, spoke out loud and clear.

'Stay *exactly* where you are!'

Mr Grimes and Mr Masterman stayed exactly where they were. Sir John slowly walked down the staircase, his shotgun never wavering.

'This time,' he announced, to Lady Harriet and the staff, who by this time were all assembled, and bearing a heterogenous selection of weapons, 'I believe we have the real villains.'

'The real villains,' said Lady Harriet.

'The real villains,' Sir John agreed. As he drew level with Mr Grimes he said calmly, 'And this time you shan't escape!'

Grimes looked at the forces and weaponry arrayed against him. He took the green gin bottle from inside his hat.

'Damn your eyes, sir, I believe you're right,' he said, and drained the bottle of its contents.

That night, Sir John held a rather special dinner party in honour of Tom's return and bravery. He invited the flower of the shire to attend, and since he was a popular and respected man, and Lady Harriet was greatly loved, everyone accepted the invitation. Harthover Hall had never seen such a glittering company assembled since the Coronation of King William IV. Mrs Tripp led Tom down the great staircase; and this time it was a Tom transmogrified. Gone were his filthy clothes. He had been carefully scrubbed all over by Mrs Tripp, and now he was as clean as he had been during his submarine adventures. He wore a silk shirt with an open collar and full sleeves, a smart, pale fawn shantung waistcoat, tight, well-fitting breeches, silk socks, and dark brown shoes with very expensive buckles. The buckles had been quickly provided by the firm of Thrubb,

Greenleaf and Gimlinge in Ilkley, and sent to Harthover haste-post-haste in a fly.

Tom sat next to Ellie, and Toby sat next to Tom. The dog had been carefully groomed by Mr Sladd for the occasion. His coat was sleek, his eyes were bright, and round his neck, instead of a collar, there was a great bow tie, fashioned from the same material that had provided Tom with his waistcoat. Altogether everyone had a very jolly time of it, though Tom and Ellie were secretly a little bored by all the adult gossip.

Eventually, when the guests had eaten their fill, Sir John rose and rapped for silence with his spoon. Then he looked across at Tom.

'On your chair, my boy. On your chair,' he said.

Tom was amazed, but Mr Sladd lifted him on to the chair, and there Tom stood, in full view.

'The time has come, young man,' Sir John told him. 'Deep breath! Don't be shy. Speak up! What we all want to know is what happened to you after you jumped into the pool. We found no trace of you. So please, tell us the full story.'

The company smiled and applauded. Tom realised that they all did genuinely want to know about his adventures. He glanced to his right, and Ellie was smiling at him encouragingly. He glanced behind him, and Mr Sladd was also beaming and nodding. He glanced to his left, and Toby was wagging his tail vigorously.

'Well,' said Tom, 'there was this lobster, but first the salmon taught me to swim and then us and the lobster went to look for the Water Babies and we met Terence – he's a seahorse – and then we were captured by the Evil Forest and then . . .'

Tom could judge an audience very well indeed. And when he had told his remarkable story he knew that his audience simply didn't understand him – or believe him. So he stopped talking suddenly, and, taking hold of Ellie's hand, ran from the dining-room.

Together, the children sprinted across the sloping lawns that led to the lake. Tom knew very well that Sir John and Lady Harriet had adopted him. He knew that his future, and Toby's, were secure. But he resented the fact that all those adults had evidently refused to accept that what he had told them, however confusedly, was true. So he and Ellie and Toby reached the waters of the lake, beautified now by moonlight.

Tom looked about him, and he thought he saw the Indian lady with no body and the old hag and Mrs Tripp and the beautiful lady in black all standing close to the sycamore that towered over the eastern shore of the lake. This strange vision enabled Tom to have courage. He knelt by the lake, and Ellie knelt also. He knew that if he could not convince Ellie that what he had experienced underwater was true, he might as well go back to chimney-sweeping. So he boldly thrust his fingers into the water, and disturbed the grave image of himself, and Ellie, and Toby, and the moon, all looking down into the lake.

There was fully one minute of silence. Then there came, from the still-disturbed waters, a voice.

'Welcome back, laddie!' Jock's voice!

'Pipeclay up the lum, dear!' came Terence's voice.

'Ees that the beautiful Ellie?' cried Claude, and Ellie blushed.

'It's good to see you again,' whispered Archie. Tom stood up, face flushed with excitement and pride.

'Now do you believe me, Ellie?'

The girl rose also. 'Oh yes. I do. I do!' she said.

Tom crowed with delight and Toby barked, and all three ran back up the lawn towards the inviting glow of Harthover Hall.